Without warning, the penguin dropped his bill and lunged into Noah. Penguin and boy crashed downward, hit the ice, and rolled into the water. Noah sank. On one side was the icy island; on the other was the long glass wall of the aquarium. He heard muffled splashes, one after another; penguins were diving in around him. They started to swim up and down the channel, churning the water.

Noah panicked and gulped freezing water. His rear end struck something—the bottom of the tank. Looking up, he could see only the white undersides of swimming penguins. He pushed up from the floor of the tank, but a penguin struck him down. Dazed, he sank a second time.

Around him, the icy water churned. He felt faint. He was exhausted. He never should have trusted Tank. Tank had said the fate of the world depended on keeping the secrets of the zoo safe. Noah's life was an easy trade.

THE SECRET ZOO

BRYAN CHICK

GREENWILLOW BOOKS
An Imprint of HarperCollinsPublishers

The Secret Zoo

Copyright © 2010 by Bryan Chick

First published in 2010 in hardcover; first paperback edition, 2011.

The text of this book is set in Arrus BT
Book design by Paul Zakris

Library of Congress Cataloging-in-Publication Data
Chick, Bryan.
The secret zoo / by Bryan Chick.
p. cm.
"Greenwillow Books."
Summary: Noah and his friends follow a trail of mysterious clues to uncover a secret behind the walls of the Clarksville City Zoo—a secret that must be protected at all costs.
ISBN 978-0-06-198750-2 (trade bdg.)
ISBN 978-0-06-198751-9 (pbk.)
[1. Mystery and detective stories. 2. Zoos—Fiction. 3. Zoo animals—Fiction. 4. Missing children—Fiction. 5. Friendship—Fiction.] I. Title.
PZ7.C4336Se 2010   [Fic]—dc22   2009042530

16 OPM 20 19 18 17 16 15

 GREENWILLOW BOOKS

FOR MY CHILDREN, STILL

✿ PRELUDE ✿

THE DISCOVERY OF A SECRET

JULY 18

Megan raced across her backyard to the tree fort. The wind snapped her pajamas, and the stiff grass pricked her bare feet. At the tree trunk, she grabbed the ladder and peered up. She could faintly see the wooden planks of the fort and, beyond them, the moon and stars. Somewhere up there, she'd left her glasses—at least, she hoped she had.

She climbed the long ladder and crawled into the fort. A glint of moonlight pulled her attention to a near corner, where she discovered her glasses lying like a big crumpled insect. She scooped them up and put them on.

"Oh! Thank you! Thank you! Thank you!" she gasped.

A sudden noise broke through the trees. It was a faint crackling sound like a piece of dry wood splintering, and it came from nearby—two or three houses down, maybe. Megan stood still and listened. A minute later, she heard the noise again, but this time it was louder—*crrraaackkk*! Then she heard a grunt, as if someone had been hurt. She ran to the wall of the fort and looked up and down the neighbors' lawns. Nothing. The dark landscape was creepy. She whistled and called her next-door neighbor's dog.

"Patches? Is that you? Are you—?"

She heard the noise again. *Crrraaackkk!* Then a thump, a thud, and another grunt.

Megan and her friends kept binoculars in the fort. She found them and balanced the lenses on her nose. Magnified, her neighborhood looked even darker than before, and the houses seemed to be trembling—until she realized that her hands were shaking.

"The zoo," she whispered.

She ran to the opposite side of the fort. The only thing separating her neighborhood from the Clarksville City Zoo was a long, winding concrete wall. From Fort Scout, she had a clear view over this wall. In daylight, she could watch the giraffes, bears, seals, and hippos as they ran, swam, and lazed about. She steadied the binoculars and stared into the zoo. Lampposts illumined the paths, but the exhibits were too dark to see.

She heard the crushing sound again and realized that it wasn't coming from the zoo. She dashed back to the opposite window and scanned the neighbors' yards once more. Nothing. Nothing but grassy lawns, trees, and rooftops.

The grunting echoed between the houses. Megan pushed up the binoculars so suddenly that they clinked against her glasses. Now she was more than creeped out; she was downright scared!

"C'mon, Meg," she said. "Nothing's out there. Quit freaking yourself—"

She gasped. Something *was* there! Some kind of creature was walking on a gable rooftop, three houses down.

"What is that?" she whispered.

She focused the binoculars and discovered five creatures creeping across the roof. A sixth was climbing the branches of the oak tree beside the house, making the limbs break. That was the sound she'd heard—branches breaking. Suddenly the creature leaped from the shaking tree, flew through the air, and landed on the house with the others. It stomped up to the roof peak and bounded onto the chimney.

The other five creatures were small and hunched over. Their long arms dangled at their sides, and as they walked, their shoulders rocked like a seesaw. Megan continued to watch them until she realized what they were. Monkeys! It seemed impossible. Monkeys had escaped the zoo and were climbing over a house in her neighborhood.

One monkey leaped from the edge of the rooftop. Megan had a clear view of its silhouette in front of the moon. Its feet hit the gutter of the adjacent rooftop with a clang, and the other monkeys followed, effortlessly jumping the distance between the houses.

"No," she said as she stared in disbelief. "Nunh-unh."

The monkeys jumped to the next house, and the next, and then disappeared into the shadows. Silence and stillness descended over the neighborhood.

"Noah . . ."

Megan hurried down the ladder and rushed into the house. Her older brother would know what to do. She flung open his bedroom door, startling him out of his sleep.

"Wha—?" Noah gasped. His hair stood out in all directions, reminding Megan of sunrays in a cartoon.

"Noah—outside!" she blurted out. "Quick!"

"What?"

"Now!"

She ran back through the house. Noah chased her outside. They dashed across the yard and climbed up to Fort Scout.

"What are you—?"

Megan snatched the binoculars and shoved them at her brother. "Here!"

"Here, what?"

"Look through them!" She pointed toward the rooftops. "Over there—I saw monkeys!"

"Megan!"

"I saw monkeys! On the rooftops!"

Her older brother looked her up and down. "You're nuts."

"Just see for yourself!"

Noah peered through the binoculars. He searched the landscape for more than a minute without saying a word. Then he handed the binoculars back to his sister and said, "Yep! You're nuts."

"Noah! I saw them. I'm telling you—"

He climbed down the ladder, saying, "What are you doing out here so late, anyway? You'll be *sooo* dead if Mom catches you out here." He reached the ground and turned to run toward the house, calling, "Come inside!"

Megan watched him run back into the house and close the door on the night. She turned her attention back to the rooftops and her neighbors' yards. She studied the shadowy landscape for nearly an hour, but nothing unusual happened.

"I know I saw them," she said, trying to convince herself.

She climbed down from the fort, returned to the house, dropped into bed, and stared at the ceiling.

She couldn't sleep. At two o'clock in the morning, she rolled out of bed and sat at her desk. Nervous, she drummed her fingers on the desktop and shifted her eyes. Her gaze stopped on a single book standing on its edge. A diary. A recent gift from her mother, the diary lacked its first entry. Megan snatched it up and opened to the first page. The binding was so stiff that she had to press the cover down before it would lie flat. She stared at the page. It was ridiculously colorful—red paper with purple lines and blue stars in the corners.

In class, she'd learned about brainstorming—scribbling down ideas as quickly as possible. Her teacher had said it was a way to make sense of something that was difficult to figure out. Megan grabbed a pencil, chewed on the eraser for a moment, and started to write.

Date: July 18
Time: 11:00 P.M.
I went outside because I forgot my stupid glasses in Fort Scout again. When I climbed up . . .

ᴗ   ᴗ   ᴗ

She wrote for an hour. Then she closed the diary, set it aside, turned off the light, and climbed back into bed. An hour later, she fell asleep without knowing that she'd just completed the first pages of a journal that would eventually alter the course of the world.

AFTER THE DISCOVERY
OCTOBER 2

Fourteen red-eyed leaf frogs hopped down the long zoo corridor, jumping and tumbling over one another as they scrambled forward. *Pop! Pop! Pop! Pop!* The sticky pads of their feet slapped the floor and sounded like exploding miniature firecrackers. A hundred aquariums lined the walls. Occasionally a frog leaped sideways and stuck to the glass for a few seconds.

The fourteen red-eyed leaf frogs hopped into a small exhibit at the end of the corridor—the special exhibit that a young girl had sneaked into just minutes earlier. They found exactly what they feared—nothing! The girl was gone. Three sheets of notebook paper lay on the ground—colorful red pages with purple lines and blue stars in the corners. Torn and crinkled, the pages were still fluttering as they settled on the floor.

The fourteen red-eyed leaf frogs didn't know the pages

were from the diary of a girl named Megan Nowicki, who months earlier had spotted monkeys escaping from the zoo. They stared at the pages. Then, whipping the sheets with their long, sticky tongues, three leaf frogs picked them up.

And so the story began.

❧ CHAPTER 1 ❧

THE BEGINNING

OCTOBER 23

Missing! Noah scooped up the paper and read the word a second time. He walked the rest of his street with his eyes fixed on the grainy black-and-white photograph of his sister and the word that had haunted him for three weeks: *missing!* Until recently, he'd associated the word with minor misplaced things like his keys or his baseball glove. But now it described his sister. On her way to a piano lesson three weeks earlier, Megan had stepped off the porch, walked down the street, and never been seen again. She'd simply disappeared.

In the first days after her disappearance, she was all

anyone could think about. Her picture was posted on every storefront window and telephone pole within a hundred miles. County residents had united to search for her. They'd walked hand in hand across open fields, scoured deep woods, and walked door-to-door in distant communities, hoping someone had seen her. Their search spanned days, weeks. But after three weeks, there was still no sign of Megan. And though no one said the words, people clearly had given up.

Determined to find his sister, Noah began his own search and called upon his two best friends, Ella and Richie, to help him. For most of their lives, Ella, Richie, Megan, and Noah had been members of a club called the Action Scouts. Their club was like most others. They had a fort, a name, secret passwords, and private meetings. What made the Action Scouts special was that it was *their* club, based on their unique friendship. So powerful was the scouts' friendship that they believed they were inseparable . . . and Noah, Ella, and Richie hoped this would bring Megan home.

It didn't.

Now, three weeks after Megan's disappearance, Noah found himself gazing at her picture as he walked across his backyard. Minutes ago, he'd found the flyer in the street; it had probably blown off a telephone pole.

"Meg, where are you?" he whispered.

The wind snapped the edges of the flyer. Noah gave it a final look and stuffed it into his pocket. He stopped in front of the big oak tree in his backyard. Nailed to it was a weather-beaten sign with fading paint. He'd made it years ago with Megan, Ella, and Richie. The sign read, YOU ARE NOW ENTERING FORT SCOUT! DO NOT ENTER! It might as well have read, WELCOME! NOW GO AWAY!

He stared high into the tree. Twenty feet above was Fort Scout, set in a tangle of tree limbs. It was the most elaborate tree fort he had ever seen. It had a roof, two doors, and four windows. It had three points of entry: a ladder, a rope, and a spiral staircase that circled the trunk and ended at a hole in the floor. Long rope bridges connected the fort to far-off trees.

Noah climbed the stairs and stepped into the fort. His footsteps thumped on the wooden planks. The fort was filled with stuff—tables and chairs and games and jackets. A pile of equipment lay on one of the tables: tools, batteries, and strange electrical objects that looked like metal bugs. These belonged to Richie. A whiz with gadgets, he was always working on what he claimed was high-tech spy equipment.

Noah stared out the window at the empty gray sky and heard nothing but the sound of the wind. He headed across one of the rope bridges toward a lookout platform. The bridge creaked and swayed. On the platform, he looked toward the Clarksville City Zoo. Two elephants, a giraffe, and a tiger were in his view, sleeping in their compounds. But mostly the zoo looked empty—empty and sad.

Looking down on the zoo from the height of the platform made Noah think of the night Megan had insisted she'd spotted monkeys on the rooftops. He remembered standing beside her, scanning the darkness for a sign of anything unusual. He'd seen nothing—certainly no runaway zoo animals.

From that night until the day she'd disappeared, Megan had acted differently. She'd been distant and preoccupied—like a person with a secret. Sometimes Noah had weird thoughts. Sometimes he wondered if the zoo had something to do with her disappearance. Megan, after all, had claimed she'd spotted animals escaping. Maybe she had; worse, maybe she wasn't supposed to. Perhaps she'd put herself in some kind of danger just by seeing them. Could the animals have come for her—kidnapped her—because something bad was going on at the zoo?

These were ridiculous ideas, and Noah knew it. He was stressed, and the stress was making him think crazy things. Still, if these ideas were so crazy, why did they keep coming back?

Noah looked away from the zoo. He wondered where Megan was, if she was okay, and whether she'd ever make it home. He bumped his toe on the short flagpole that lay on the platform. The flag was red with large white letters: *A* and *S*. He picked it up and held it in the air. "The Action Scouts' distress flag," he muttered.

Two years earlier, Richie's grandfather, an army veteran, had given the kids the idea of making distress flags. He'd said that if the scouts became separated, they'd need a way to communicate trouble, and the distress flags had been his answer. He talked Richie's grandmother into making one for each of the children and one for Fort Scout.

Noah fitted the pole into a spot in the tree. The flag waved, and the *A* and *S* rippled in the breeze. He looked across his yard and into the street. A part of him hoped Ella or Richie would see the flag and come running. If not Ella or Richie, then someone—anyone—who could help him get back his sister and his old life.

Noah waited almost a half hour. No one came. Finally the cold got the best of him.

He climbed down from Fort Scout, entered the house, and went to bed early. As he lay beneath the covers, he imagined Megan, her warm smile and her sisterly love. Eventually he drifted to sleep.

Shortly before midnight, he woke to a *Tap! Tap! Tap!* on his bedroom window.

CHAPTER 2

A CRYPTIC MESSAGE

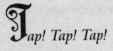*ap! Tap! Tap!*

Noah sat up, glanced around the dimly lit room, and listened. Had he imagined it? *Tap! Tap! Tap!* The sound came again.

He jumped out of bed. "Who's there?" he called.

Tap! Tap! the window answered.

He crept across the floor, not knowing what he might find. Was a branch rapping his window? Could a loose shutter be rattling?

Tap! Tap! Tap!

He stood at the window and peered out. He saw

nothing but the black, starlit sky. No branch, no loose shutter—nothing.

Tap! Tap!

He strained his eyes to see better, but all he saw was the night.

Tap! Tap! Tap! Tap!

He swung open the window. The cool air brushed his skin, and goose bumps rose along his arms. A bird had perched on the window ledge. Barely the size of his thumb, it had shiny blue feathers and a bright red bill. As it looked at Noah, it tipped its head from side to side inquisitively.

Relief washed over the boy from head to toe. "You scared me half to—"

The bird sprang off the ledge, flew into his room, and circled near the ceiling.

"Hey!" Noah shouted. "Get outta here!"

The bird fluttered around for several seconds before it perched on a lampshade near the bed. It snapped its head back and forth, staring at Noah as if it expected something.

"Out!" Noah ordered. "Get out!"

Then, as suddenly as the bird had flown into the room, it lifted off the lampshade, dived through the window, and flew out—all in the blink of an eye.

"Good!"

Noah brushed his hands together, happy to be done with the bird. But as he walked toward the window to close it, the winged creature darted back in.

"Get out, I said!"

The bird continuously circled near the ceiling. Each time it veered overhead, Noah jumped up and tried to snag it out of the air. After his fifth or sixth jump, he noticed that the bird was clutching something in its tiny talons— a piece of paper. A moment later, the bird dropped the paper into the hollow of Noah's pillow, headed for the window, and perched on the sill.

Puzzled, Noah stared at the bird. He watched its beady eyes dart from his face to the paper, reminding him of the way his grandmother would restlessly wait for someone to unwrap a present. Its expression said, *Well? This was given to you for a reason!*

The paper on his pillow was wrinkled and torn, and it looked as though it had spent a week in a puddle. He picked it up and flattened the creases to reveal a funny-looking monkey with bushy eyebrows, a tuft of hair growing on its chin, and a long tail. The heading above the photo read, "Come to the Clarksville City Zoo and See Our New Friend, Mr. Tall Tail!"

Noah had seen Mr. Tall Tail at the zoo many times. He certainly wasn't a new arrival. This was an old flyer.

"What's going on?" Noah turned toward the bird. "What's—?"

The bird was gone.

Noah looked back at the paper. Mr. Tall Tail stared at him with wide, worried eyes. Noah read it again: "Come to the Clarksville City Zoo and See Our New Friend, Mr. Tall Tail!"

This is nothing. It's trash that a bird picked up, Noah told himself.

But he had read about birds acting as messengers and delivering notes to people.

"Don't be dumb," Noah muttered. "We have e-mail these days. Besides, this paper doesn't have a message. There's not a—"

He peered at the heading. A few of the words had holes in them—tiny holes that looked as if someone had punched them out with the tip of a pencil. Or maybe with the tip of a tiny beak.

"No way . . ."

He read out loud only the words with holes: "To the Clarksville City Zoo and Our New Friend." It made no sense.

"Wait a minute!" He scanned the words *without* holes in them. "Come . . . See . . . Mr. . . . Tall . . . Tail."

Was this a message?

"No," he mumbled. "It can't be." He read the new

sentence again, without pausing between the words. "Come see Mr. Tall Tail."

The sentence was complete, structured—even instructional.

Noah raised his eyes to the window. The sill was empty. The wind blew gentle ripples through his ivory-colored drapes. He shivered. The drapes looked like ghosts.

CHAPTER 3

A TALE OF WONDER

The school bell rang and Noah raced for the door, not bothering to slow down when Mrs. Bluss called, "Kids! Walk!" Noah didn't have time for walking. He only had three hours before his parents would be home, so he needed to move fast.

Since Megan's disappearance, Noah's parents had been working late, leading a search campaign out of a friend's office in downtown Clarksville. Considering all that his parents had been through with Megan, they'd originally had concerns about Noah's walking home from school and being by himself at the house. They'd finally decided to allow it, as long as Noah promised to walk home with his friends. And rather than being home by himself, Noah almost always stayed at Richie's until his parents picked him up after leaving the search headquarters for the day.

Today, however, Noah needed to break the rules. In the hallway, he tossed his books into his locker, scanned the crowd to make sure Ella and Richie couldn't see him, and then squirmed his way to the main exit. Outside, he ran across the schoolyard, kicking up gravel and dust.

He hadn't slept since the bird's strange visit the previous night. He still couldn't make sense of what had happened. Did it mean something, or had a bird simply flown through his window and dropped a piece of trash in his room? Whatever it might be, there would be no harm in paying Mr. Tall Tail a visit.

He walked down the drive, turned onto Jenkins Street, and walked alongside the concrete wall of the zoo. After rounding the corner onto Walkers Boulevard, he reached the zoo and bolted for the entrance, where he flashed his membership card to a startled attendant and crashed through the turnstile.

Because the day was so cold, the zoo was nearly empty. Noah stormed across the pavement, weaving in and out of the exhibits. He'd been to the zoo so many times that he knew the shortest path to the langur house without thinking about it. When he reached the small, ivy-draped building, he pushed through the entrance, turned a corner, and nearly crashed into a small group of people.

The exhibit had no traditional bars or concrete walls. An enormous dome-shaped net kept the langurs inside, where they relaxed on trees, looking bored. Their tails were so long that Noah wondered how the animals managed to keep them from becoming knotted in the branches. Mr. Tall Tail had the longest tail of all. As the monkey rested on a high branch, his tail dangled below his rear end like a furry snake.

Now that Noah was inside the exhibit, he felt a bit foolish. What did he expect to see?

The visitors gradually wandered off, and the building fell silent. The langurs turned their eyes toward Noah occasionally, but they showed little interest in him.

"Psssttt!" Noah said. "Mr. Tall Tail!"

The monkey ignored him. He was more interested in a large leaf that was trapped in the ceiling of the net.

"Mr. Tall Tail! Can you hear me?"

The monkey picked a closer leaf, popped it in his mouth, and chewed casually.

"Um . . . okay," Noah muttered, scratching his head. "Why am I talking to a monkey?"

The entrance door swung open, and a security guard stepped inside. He had a thatch of fire engine red hair and plump lips, and his face and arms were covered in freckles.

"Hello," Noah said, feeling stupid and embarrassed. After all, this man had nearly caught him talking to a monkey.

The guard didn't answer, and an awkward silence filled the air. He strolled past Noah, observing him skeptically. Noah stared at the langurs, pretending that he was enjoying himself. The sound of the guard's footsteps softened as he rounded the exhibit. Finally Noah heard the exit door open and close. He was alone again with the langurs.

"Talk about creepy," Noah mumbled.

He glanced at Mr. Tall Tail once more and said, "Nothing to show me, huh?"

Mr. Tall Tail stared into space and idly chewed his leaf, working his jaw from side to side.

Feeling like an idiot, Noah decided to leave and turned toward the exit. At that moment, something fell on his shoulder, and in a reflex reaction, Noah swatted his back. He swung around and yelped. A long, black, furry thing slithered across his forearm. It jumped off and floated in the air. Then Noah realized what it was—Mr. Tall Tail's tail!

Seeing Noah turn to leave, the langur had leaped to the front of the net, deliberately poked out his tail, and brushed it over Noah's shoulder. What's more, a slip of paper was wrapped in the tip. Noah knew it was crazy, but Mr. Tall Tail was handing him the paper.

The monkey waved his tail as if to say, *Are you gonna take this, or what?*

Noah crept forward. He reached out his trembling arm and snatched the paper.

"What is this?" he said.

Mr. Tall Tail leaped back up to the trees and relaxed in his previous spot in the branches. He picked another leaf and chewed. His dark eyes gazed blankly into the distance, as if nothing had happened.

For a second, Noah thought he'd imagined the whole incident, but the paper was in his hand—crumpled, ripped, and spotted. A few langur hairs even clung to it. Noah opened it carefully. The moment he saw the message inside, he thought he'd faint.

The front door creaked open again, and he thrust the paper into his pocket. For the second time, the redheaded security guard walked in. He eyed Noah suspiciously, and as he approached, his heels angrily smacked the floor. What Noah had read on the paper was making his stomach roll and his head ache.

"You okay, kid? You ain't lookin' too hot," the guard said.

"Yeah . . . fine." Noah was anything *but* fine. He could barely breathe. "I gotta go," he managed to say.

He hurried for the door, slammed through it, and burst into the cool air.

"Have a nice day," the guard called out.

The door crashed as it closed. Gasping, Noah leaned against a wall. He pulled out the paper and looked at it again. It was red with purple lines and blue stars in the corners. He'd seen it before.

"Deep breaths," he told himself. "It's okay . . . it's okay . . . it's okay. . . ."

But even as he repeated the words, he didn't believe them for a second.

⟡ CHAPTER 4 ⟡

A Mysterious Clue
to a Mysterious Zoo

Noah sat on a bench in a quiet part of the zoo. He glanced over both shoulders to make sure nobody was around and pulled Mr. Tall Tail's paper out of his pocket. Neat cursive handwriting covered every inch. All the letters were joined by smooth arcs, and the dots on the *i*'s were carefully placed. Though the ink was faded and smeared, he knew the penmanship. It was Megan's. There was no mistaking it.

Noah glanced around again; still, no one was nearby. A wind swept across the zoo. Noah took a breath, gathered his courage, and read the page. It started in the middle of a sentence.

keep seeing birds in the Forest of Flight exhibit that aren't supposed to be there. A bird chart near the entrance has a "complete list" of birds, but a few that I see aren't even on it. Then, every few days, some of those birds aren't around anymore. On top of that, an old lady who works there keeps following me around, asking me what I'm doing. She's creepy.

The bottom of the page was missing. Noah flipped it over. The writing at the top was too smeared to read. The words he could decipher began in the middle of a sentence and the middle of a new thought.

can't write it down without feeling stupid—but I know what I saw!

There's a wall with holes in it. I think the holes are supposed to give the birds a private place to build their nests. They're supposed to be like cracks and crannies in rocks and mountains and stuff. I got curious. I found a bench near the wall and sat there awhile, pretending to read a pamphlet. After an hour or so, I saw something! There was a bunch

The page was torn. Noah flipped the paper over repeatedly, hoping to find something in the margins.

He dropped against the back of the bench and stared into space. What was going on? What did all this mean? Why had Megan been making trips to the zoo without informing the family? And how had a langur got hold of a page from her diary?

Noah's first instinct was to tell somebody. An adult at the zoo. But Megan had been suspicious of the zoo worker—and hadn't he just had a strange encounter with a security guard? What did all this mean?

The leaves fell around him like colorful snowflakes. He was stunned and confused.

"I don't get it," he muttered. "I don't get it at all."

But one thing Noah did understand was that he had to act—and he had to act quickly. In two hours, the zoo would close. That would be more than enough time to take a tour of the Forest of Flight and perhaps to examine the wall with the unusual crannies and holes.

CHAPTER 5

Investigating the Forest of Flight

The Forest of Flight exhibit was in a building that stood forty feet high. Because of its enormous dome roof, the building always made Noah think of a giant igloo. The walls and roof were made of the same tinted glass that was used on the windows of fancy cars. The exhibit was open; people could walk among freely flying birds.

The moment Noah strolled through the entrance, the earthy smell of soil and tree bark invaded him. Trees and flowery plants filled the dome with fragrance and rich oxygen. Small waterfalls cascaded down rocks and threw mist into the air. The Forest of Flight looked and felt like a miniature jungle. Birds soared overhead, and a variety of sounds echoed off the walls—water splashing, children laughing, streams rumbling, and birds chirping and squawking.

A poster with a chart was pinned to the wall near the entrance, displaying pictures of fifty different birds, just as Megan had described. Noah stopped for a minute to search the chart. Halfway down, he recognized one of the birds and gasped. It had a blue body, a bright red bill, and an orange belly. Without doubt, this was the tiny bird that had flown into his room. The chart said it was a malachite kingfisher named Marlo.

"Marlo," Noah said aloud. He looked to the treetops. "Marlo, are you in here?"

He headed down a misty path, where enormous umbrella leaves draped above him like a live green ceiling. Droplets of water plopped on his shoulders and the top of his head. Around him, a variety of birds perched on branches and steel beams, while a few floated on streams and ponds and others pecked at seeds on the ground, looking more bored than hungry.

Noah scoured the Forest of Flight for Marlo but couldn't find him. His search led him to a concrete wall—the wall that had the holes in it, which was what he'd come to see. The holes were about ten feet up from the ground and eight inches across. They were dark—the kind of dark that someone could keep secrets in.

Noah took a seat on the bench that Megan had written about. He folded his hands across his lap and said under his breath, "This is where Megan sat not long ago." The thought of her sitting here alone made him sad.

Noah watched the wall and waited . . . and waited . . . and waited. Birds flew in and out of the holes. One had a beak full of straw, and Noah guessed that it was building a nest. He continued to sit and watch. An hour later, a voice announced through a loudspeaker that the zoo was preparing to close. Within minutes, people had cleared out of the Forest of Flight. Noah was alone. If something significant was going to take place, he thought it might be now.

More time passed. Except for the chirps and fluttering of the birds, the building was silent. Now that Noah was alone in the building, it seemed larger than ever. Through the glass walls, he watched the sky dim as the sun fell into its autumn slumber. Noah began to worry that he might be locked in the zoo for the night.

Suddenly a tiny bird swooped down and perched on a branch directly in front of him. It had a blue body, a red beak, and an orange belly.

"Marlo?"

The bird cocked his head, first to one side and then to the other. He ruffled his feathers and blinked so many times in a split second that Noah couldn't count the blinks.

The boy rose from the bench. "Marlo, do you . . . do you understand me?"

Marlo cocked his head back and forth again and leaped into the air. He circled a clump of trees and landed back on the branch in front of Noah.

Noah's jaw dropped. He glanced over his shoulder. As far as he could tell, he was alone—alone with Marlo.

"This is really happening," he said.

Marlo sprang off the branch and left it trembling. He darted through the air and disappeared into one of the holes.

How deep are those things? Noah wondered. He stepped forward, wrapped his hands around a rail, and locked his gaze on the hole, waiting.

"C'mon, Marlo," he mumbled. "The zoo's gotta be closing, and I—"

Marlo shot out of the hole, etched another circle in the air, and landed on an open branch. Noah's attention bounced between the bird and the hole. A minute later, another bird darted out. This one was green with a yellow beak.

The idea occurred to Noah that he should be taking notes the way Megan had done. He plucked a pen from his jacket and wrote, on the edge of Megan's notepaper, "Marlo" and "green bird."

A few minutes later, a bird with long wings emerged from the hole. Under "green bird," Noah wrote "bird—long wings." A fourth and fifth bird flew from the hole. Noah simply scrawled the numbers 4 and 5.

He waited, keeping his gaze fixed on the wall and his pen poised on the paper, but nothing happened. He started to wonder whether anything more than this was going to take place. Five birds had appeared, but they seemed insignificant.

All of a sudden, more birds shot out of the hole, each one directly on the tail of the bird ahead of it. They were flying so close to one another that they blurred together in a stream of colorful feathers. In a matter of seconds, hundreds of birds filled the Forest of Flight. They dived through the treetops, perched on the branches, and skimmed the glass walls. Their wings made so much noise that Noah dropped Megan's paper and plugged his ears. He felt as though he was in a dream—a dream that was at once strange and magnificent and terrifying.

"What's *haaapppennniiinggg*?" he hollered.

He closed his eyes and braced himself for what would be next. The birds flew around him, fanning his skin with mild gusts of wind, making him feel as if he were standing in the center of a tiny tornado. The experience was exciting and frightening. He didn't know if he should scream in panic or scream in delight, so he just screamed, "*Aaahhh!*"

Chirping, whistling, squawking, and cawing, the birds circled him and filled the Forest of Flight with their strange musical chatter. Their feathers brushed his cheeks. Noah had no sense of how much time was passing. Several seconds? Or many minutes? He became certain that he would be carried off, that the birds would try to squeeze him into the hole in the wall and take him to some unknown place. But a moment later, the noises stopped and the air became still. Noah heard only the gurgling streams and splashing waterfalls.

He opened his eyes. Leaves and feathers floated around him like ash from a campfire. He looked up at the hole just in time to see the last few birds plunge back into it. As effortlessly as they had filled the exhibit, they had exited. Those that had been there throughout the day went about their normal business, circling treetops and munching seeds. The hole in the wall looked ordinary. A bird coasted out of it, snatched some twigs, and flew back inside.

"Wait! Marlo!" Noah scanned the treetops. He saw no sign of the bird. "Marlo! What happened? I—"

The sound of footsteps rose in the distance. A man with a ball-shaped belly plodded up to Noah, wagging his finger and saying, "Young man! What are you doing here? The zoo's closing!"

"Excuse me?" Noah said. He snatched up Megan's note and slipped it into a pocket in his pants.

"You wanna get locked in here? Come with me! Let's go!"

The man scanned the exhibit. Noah saw his eyes rest briefly on the hole in the wall. He put his hand on the boy's back and escorted him to the door.

Once outside, Noah rushed toward the zoo exit. He was so confused that he felt sick. So much had happened in just a few hours. He pushed through the clutches of the turnstile, raced across the parking lot, and ran down the sidewalk next to Walkers Boulevard.

At his house, he dropped on the couch and sat almost without moving until his parents returned home. He spent the evening in a daze and went to bed before dark. Night fell, but he was unable to sleep. He lay in bed, scanning the shadows in the half-moon light that filtered through the window, thinking about the events at the zoo. His gaze happened upon his jacket, which he'd tossed onto a chair. He saw something sticking out of the pocket— something he hadn't put there. He climbed out of bed, walked to the chair, thrust his hand into the pocket, and pulled out a piece of crumpled paper. This time, it was exactly what he expected—another note from his sister. During the commotion at the Forest of Flight, a bird must have slipped it into his pocket.

He smoothed out the paper and sat on his bed to read it.

When he finished, he clutched it to his chest and declared, "I cannot do this alone."

He knew he had to find help. That meant it was time to round up the bravest kids he knew. It was time to call on the Action Scouts.

⚙ CHAPTER 6 ⚙

SHARING A SECRET

At school the next day, Noah could barely function. At lunchtime, he took a seat at the end of a long table in the cafeteria and waited for his friends. He slouched over his tray and picked through his food as if he expected to find something buried in it. Around him, kids behaved in their normal fashion: laughing, hollering, and launching corn with their plastic spoon catapults.

A girl plopped down on the bench in front of him. She landed so hard that she shook the Tater Tot off Becky Prebee's spork at the far end of the bench. The girl was

Ella Jones, Noah's lifelong friend and fellow Action Scout.

Noah looked up from his meal and stared at her blankly.

"What's up?" she asked as she crunched down on an apple, spraying droplets of juice for which she saw no need to apologize. When Noah didn't respond, she added, "Cat got your tongue?" Because she was talking through a mouthful of food, her question sounded like "Cagotyoton?"—as if she were speaking some foreign language.

Noah said coldly, "Nice manners. Shouldn't you be eating off the floor?"

Ella chuckled. "Ha! Woof-woof!" Through another mouthful of food, she said something else that Noah couldn't understand. It sounded remarkably like "I have a toad in my shoe."

"Hey, guys!"

Behind him, Noah heard the voice of the third Action Scout. Richie Reynolds approached the table wearing his favorite shirt, a green one with shiny silver snaps. His pockets contained a stash of pens, a pencil, two highlighters, a short ruler, and a penlight. Ella called this stuff Richie's nerd-gear.

Richie stretched his leg over the bench to take a seat. For a second, light reflected off the metallic material in his running shoe, causing colored flecks of light to crawl across Noah's arm. Richie's running shoes were so flashy and bright and glittery that they were obnoxious. Noah could spot them from the end of a crowded school hall. Richie wore these shoes everywhere—to school, to baseball practice, even to church. When his skinny rear end hit the bench, his oversized eyeglasses shook and became crooked.

Richie pushed his glasses up on his nose, looked at his food, rubbed his hands together, and said, "Mmm. . . . I can't wait to dig into this." He prodded through his lunch with a plastic spork. "This—this is . . . What is this stuff? Chicken?"

"I'm afraid to guess," Ella said. She peeled a banana and added, "Something's wrong with Noah today."

"Nothing's wrong," Noah said, but even he could hear how cold and flat his voice sounded.

"Doesn't sound like nothing's wrong," Richie replied.

"I didn't sleep well."

"Why not?"

Noah stared into the ugly mound of food on his tray and avoided the question.

Richie continued to dig through his lunch, trying to determine what category of meat was on the tray.

"Looks like something's been rocking Noah's ark," Richie said. "Maybe the animals have been keeping him awake."

Noah coughed up a piece of food. It landed on the table with a *splat*.

"Whoa!" Ella said. She reached across the table and touched his arm, looking concerned.

Richie said, "Sorry, Noah. I was only joking."

"It's okay. It's just that . . ."

"Just that what?" Ella asked.

"Nothing."

"C'mon! How long have we been friends?" she said.

Noah didn't know why, but he was finding it difficult to tell them about the zoo. He reminded himself that he trusted his friends more than anyone else in the world.

He gathered his courage and blurted out, "It's Megan!"

Ella and Richie turned serious. There was no joking between them when the subject was Megan.

"What is it?" Ella asked.

"I—" He stopped and stared into space.

"Noah," Ella said, "you can tell us anything."

Knowing that this was true—that these two were the best friends anyone could ever hope for—Noah let his eyes meet Ella's and said, "The animals at the zoo . . . I think . . . no . . . I *know* they have something to do with Megan's disappearance."

Ella's jaw fell. Richie dropped a piece of the unidentified meat. For a moment, the three of them sat and stared at one another, not knowing what to say next. Then Noah glanced over both shoulders to make sure no one was watching them.

"Look at this," he said. "I have to show you something."

He thrust his hand into his pocket to find Megan's notes.

⁕ CHAPTER 7 ⁕

BLIZZARD CONDITIONS

That afternoon, Noah met Ella and Richie inside the zoo entrance, beside the water fountain. The weather was unusually cold for October. Ella wore fluffy pink earmuffs that looked like big globs of cotton candy stuck to her ears. Richie wore his favorite winter hat, a stocking cap with a ribbed cuff and a large red pom-pom on top. The pom-pom shook whenever Richie moved.

"You guys ready for this?" Noah asked.

Ella winked and smiled at Noah. Richie nodded his head—and his pom-pom.

Ella said, "Let's check out that note again—the one the birds gave you."

They found a private spot beneath a tree. Noah opened the crumpled paper, and the three children focused on the page. The writing started in the middle of a sentence and the middle of a thought, as it did on the note that Mr. Tall Tail had given him.

> *too much going on, too much I don't understand. I'm sooo confused! I've been investigating the underwater tunnel at the Polar Pool in Arctic Town. The lady who works there always watches me as if she suspects something. It's creepy! She always asks if I'm with my parents, and I just say yes.*

Ella turned to Noah and asked, "Did you know she was coming here?"

"Nunh-unh!"

"Those piano lessons she was taking with Ms. Courtney—you know, the ones over the summer—I bet if we check into that—" Ella stopped herself, realizing that she was about to call Megan a liar.

Noah finished her thought, saying, "I bet she can't even play 'Chopsticks.'"

They exchanged a knowing look and turned their attention back to Megan's note.

Anyway, I need to get home. Noah's probably home already, and I'm supposed to be there. I'll tell him and the other scouts about this soon. But right now, they'd probably think I'm crazy.

All for now.

Megan

P.S. Almost forgot! I have to remember to watch the polar bears when the zoo starts to close. They get real active. It's best to watch them from the glass tunnel—especially around the Polar Pool's curves and corners. I know I saw light coming

The writing ended. Noah turned the paper over. The second side was too smeared to read anything except a few lines:

only has two polar bears, Frosty and Blizzard. But if I saw what I think I saw, this whole thing is getting really weird.

For a second I saw three bears! Is that possible? I was

That was the end of the back of the page.

Richie said, "Wait . . . the zoo only has two polar bears."

"Yeah," Noah said. "And it's only supposed to have fifty birds—not thousands."

The scouts stood together in silence. The wind blew Megan's note, making it flutter and snap in Noah's hand.

"This is real, isn't it?" Ella asked.

"Yeah," Noah said. "This is really happening."

"C'mon," Richie said as he settled the wiggly pom-pom on his cap. His voice sounded unusually courageous. "Let's go to the tunnel and see how many bears we find."

They turned and headed deeper into the zoo.

Arctic Town was an area of the zoo designed to look like a cold Arctic landscape. From the concession stands to the restrooms, all the buildings were shaped like igloos. Plastic icicles dangled from every ledge, sheets of plastic ice lay across the sidewalks, and signs cautioned visitors, WATCH FOR ICE ON PATH! The design had a cool effect in winter, but a rather lame one in summer. Could children believe it was cold when snow cones were melting down their fingers?

In no time, the scouts reached the Polar Pool. Set on an icy-looking landscape, the exhibit had a long, winding inground pool. A flight of narrow stairs descended twenty feet into the earth and led to a glass-walled underwater tunnel, which reached across the middle of the pool.

"Let's go," Noah said.

They rushed down the stairs and stepped into a glass room that looked into the pool. Though this room had a spectacular view, the real attraction was the tunnel. It started at the room they were in, snaked through the water, and opened into a second glass room at the other end, which was barely visible from here. It was like a hamster's plastic tunnel, but a thousand times larger.

The scouts strolled into the tunnel; they felt as if they were walking directly into the pool. Inside the tunnel, they joined a bunch of kids who were watching Blizzard. The bear was trying to sink an orange barrel with his thick legs, which moved sluggishly through the water. He was enormous. After a while, Frosty started to wrestle with Blizzard. A few minutes passed, and Blizzard swam over the tunnel, casting his shadow over the visitors beneath him. He planted his paw on the glass directly above Richie. It was bigger than Richie's head.

The scouts stared into the tank, hoping to catch sight of something unusual—a third bear, perhaps—but they saw nothing. Noah suggested that it was too early for anything weird to happen. To kill time, they decided to leave the tunnel and have a snack at one of the igloo concession stands upstairs.

On their way, Richie pretended to slip on a patch of fake ice that had spilled across the sidewalk.

"Hey, guys!" he called. *"Whooaaa!"*

His arms flailed and the pom-pom on his cap wobbled. About twenty seconds into his routine, he lost his balance and crashed on his butt.

"Richie!" Ella said. "If you don't knock it off, we're gonna put you in with the monkeys."

Richie climbed to his feet and rubbed his sore rear end.

After wasting an hour, they returned to the Polar Pool, made their way into the tunnel, and waited anxiously for something to happen. Before long, a lady announced through a loudspeaker that the zoo would close in fifteen minutes. Parents collected their children and headed for the exit. Within minutes, the Action Scouts were the only ones left in the tunnel.

"Megan said it happened late in the day," Noah said. "And that's when all that stuff with the birds happened to me."

"Yeah," Ella said.

Frosty and Blizzard swam at one end of the pool, their massive paws deftly slicing the water.

"See anything unusual?" Noah asked.

"Nunh-unh," Richie said.

The three children stood with their faces pressed against the tunnel wall. Their breath clouded the glass. Silence hung in the air and time passed.

Then, out of nowhere, Richie said, "I got a joke."

"What?" Ella moaned.

"A joke! I got a joke."

Without looking away from the pool, Noah said, "Go ahead."

"Ready?" Richie asked.

"For crying out loud," Ella said, "stalling isn't going to make it funnier."

Richie cleared his throat and said, "What's white and furry and shaped like a tooth?"

"What's *what*?"

"What's white . . . and furry . . . and shaped like a tooth?"

"I don't know," Noah said. "What?"

"A molar bear!"

No one laughed. Noah and Ella just stood and peered into the water.

"A molar bear," Richie repeated. "Don't you guys get it?"

"Of course we get it," Ella said. "We're just not six anymore."

"Geez," Richie said. "I guess—"

"Quiet!" Noah said. "I see something!"

"What? Where?" Richie said.

"Light! I saw light!"

Noah had seen a beam of light inside the pool, but it had come from the bottom of the tank.

"I don't see anything," Ella said. "Where?"

"It was out there, but only for a second. A ray of light—just like the light that Megan described!" Noah said.

"You sure it wasn't coming from the sky?" Richie asked.

"No, it wasn't!"

The next moment, the scouts heard a high-pitched sound coming from the room behind them—the room they'd entered the tunnel from. It sounded like a big metal door opening. They turned in the direction of the noise.

"What was that?" Ella whispered.

"I don't know," Noah said. "Maybe someone who works here."

They pushed away from the glass and tried to act casual. Ella fluffed her ponytail, and Richie ruffled the pom-pom on his cap. The scouts heard another high-pitched sound, followed by the sound of something slamming shut.

"That's too loud to be a normal door," Richie whispered.

Suddenly, through the layers of glass that formed the winding tunnel, the scouts saw movement. Something had entered the room. Something big. And white.

From where she stood, Ella could see around the corner. A moment later, her face turned pale.

"Uh . . . guys?"

A new sound filled the exhibit: *wwwrrrooooowwwlll*!

"What is it?" Noah said.

Before she could reply, the head of a huge polar bear emerged at the opening of the tunnel. The bear snarled, swung its snout from side to side, and fixed its black eyes on the scouts.

Noah tried to say something, but only a flat, meaningless sound came out. "Unnnhhh . . ."

The bear threw back its head and roared. Its tongue looked like a slab of meat. Its ivory fangs were razor sharp.

Noah glanced into the pool. Only one bear was out there. It was Frosty, the smaller bear, which meant this was Blizzard. Somehow Blizzard had entered the tunnel.

The scouts stood frozen in place. Noah's friends looked like statues with goofy headgear—one with fluffy earmuffs and the other with a stocking cap.

Ella nervously broke the silence, whispering, "Hey, Richie, any good jokes we can tell it?"

"Don't move," Noah warned. "Just keep perfectly still."

Blizzard stepped out of the room and into the tunnel. Water dribbled off his fur and formed large puddles on the floor. He closed to within ten feet of the children and rolled his daunting head.

"The room behind us—it has an exit," Noah said.

"Richie, can we run faster than this thing?" Ella whispered.

"I don't know," he replied.

Blizzard swung his head around at Noah and growled. Noah carefully eyed the bear. Suddenly a strange calm swept over him.

"Hold on a minute." He stepped forward and said cautiously, "Blizzard? Um . . . hi."

The bear inched down the tunnel.

"What are you *doing*?" Ella asked.

Noah reached out. His hand was trembling. "Shh! This will work," he said.

Blizzard nudged his head against Noah's open palm. His fur was coarse, wet, and cold. He sniffed Noah's arm, and his coal-black nose left a wet spot on Noah's jacket. Noah realized how massive Blizzard was. His legs were like tree trunks, and his head was as big as a beach ball. Noah stroked Blizzard's crown as the bear sniffed his arm.

"Blizzard," he said, "do you know who I am? I'm Noah."

Blizzard growled softly.

"It's okay, guys," Noah said. "He's here to help us—like the other animals."

"This is crazy," Ella said.

Ella and Richie crept forward. When they reached Blizzard, they gingerly placed their palms on his side.

"What's going on?" Richie asked. "How can this be happening?"

"I have no idea," Noah admitted.

"How did he get in here?"

"There's something in that first room—a door or something. Remember that noise we heard?" Noah said.

"This is like a dream," Ella said.

In a flash, the entrance door opened, and through the glass walls, Noah detected light from outside filling the staircase. A man was speaking.

". . . yeah . . . yeah. Right. I know. I gotta pick up the . . ."

Noah could faintly see a zoo employee. He was propping the door open with his hip while he talked to another person nearby.

Blizzard grunted and looked at the scouts. He dropped something from his mouth—a wadded-up ball of paper. Noah scooped it up. It was wet and gooey with spit. He crammed it into his pocket, and Blizzard thundered back down the tunnel. The floor quaked.

". . . need to pick up my toolbox," the zoo attendant was saying. "That's a big headache we got down there. We'll need to . . ."

When Blizzard reached the end of the tunnel, he turned the corner and disappeared. Seconds later, the scouts heard the loud, high-pitched sound that they'd heard earlier. That was it, then; Blizzard had entered the exhibit through some kind of secret door.

"First I gotta close up the tunnel," the man continued. "Let me do a walk-through real quick. I'll meet you on the platform."

The door snapped shut. Through the glass, Noah saw the man approaching.

"Don't say anything," Noah said. "If Blizzard doesn't trust this guy, we don't, either."

"Totally," Ella agreed.

The man turned into the tunnel. When he saw the scouts, he waved his fingertips toward himself and said, "Let's go, kids. I gotta lock up this joint."

"It's that late already?" Noah asked casually.

"Yeah, yeah. Zoo's closing. C'mon, let's speed it up."

As the children scurried around the zoo attendant, he glanced at the floor.

"What's this?" he said. "The floor's soaked! What did you kids spill?"

They stood in silence, stunned.

The man lowered his eyebrows and said, "Ahhh, forget it! C'mon, now. The three of ya—get!" He accompanied them up the stairs.

As the scouts were walking off, he said, "Wait!"

Noah turned his head and saw the man's finger pointed at him.

"Don't I know you?"

"Nunh-unh," Noah replied.

"I'm sure I've seen you before."

"I doubt it."

Scratching his chin, the man looked him over. Finally he said, "Yeah, well, whatever. The three of you—get on now."

As they hurried off, Ella said, "Noah, he knows who you are!"

"Yeah," Noah said. "And I'll bet you anything he knows who my sister is, too."

They ran toward the zoo exit. Noah reached into his pocket to make sure the paper Blizzard had given him was still there. It was. That meant the scouts had more reading to do.

❧ CHAPTER 8 ❧

CREEPY CRITTERS

After school the next day, the scouts raced down Walkers Boulevard toward the zoo. Once inside, they ran toward the back, dodging benches and cutting through buildings as they headed for an exhibit called Creepy Critters. Creepy Critters had over three hundred aquariums of different sizes, shapes, and purposes. Each aquarium held things that were slimy or scaly or hairy or generally creepy in some regard—things like snakes, lizards, spiders, fish, and even cockroaches as big and thick as adult thumbs.

In no time, the scouts crossed the zoo and entered the

exhibit. Creepy Critters had a bizarre design. The building seemed to be a hapless collection of zigzagging hallways. Aquariums were set in every wall, and it felt as if the building was made of giant glass bricks. The concrete spots between the aquariums were covered in fake slime, mold, webs, and cocoons. Plastic vines and goopy gunk dangled from the ceiling.

Children raced alongside the aquariums, pausing at each one just long enough to peer inside and leave fingerprints on the glass. Their parents strolled behind them with bundles of jackets slung over their arms. Sounds rebounded from the hard glass walls like noises in a cave.

The scouts found a spot on an open bench. The aquarium in front of them was filled with tiny bright pink frogs resting on branches and mossy rocks—splotches of color on a green canvas.

"Okay, Noah," Richie said. "Let's see that note from Blizzard again."

Noah pulled the crinkled note from his pocket and smoothed it against his knee. He read aloud.

> *and I hardly believe it—even after seeing it myself. It's as if my mind doesn't want to believe what I saw. Does that make sense? It makes sense when I write it, and I guess that's all that matters. But I wish I knew better words*

and could describe things better. I wish I had
Richie's big brain.

"Finally," Richie said as he tapped his finger on the page. "A person who knows genius when she sees it."

"Quiet, Richie," Ella said. "This is important."

Noah turned the page over.

Anyway, none of that matters because I'll sort
this out later. What matters is what I saw in
Creepy Critters today. There's an exhibit called
the Chamber of Lights. It's at the end of a long
hall. It's nothing but a dark room the size of
a closet. There's a big aquarium in there filled
with tiny fish. The fish are called flashlight
fish and they blink like fireflies. Today I saw
someone

The page ended. Noah stuffed the note back into his pocket.

"Well," he said, "what do you guys make of that?"

"Something important is obviously in that exhibit," Ella said.

"But what?" Richie asked.

"There's one way to find out," Noah said, rising to his feet.

He was a single step down the hall when he stopped and fixed his eyes on the aquarium that housed the pink frogs.

"Guys, look!" he said.

Lined up along the window, side by shiny pink side, the frogs were crowding the front of the aquarium. A few remained perched along the branches, but even those were staring directly at the scouts.

Ella gasped and inched to the window, sliding the flats of her feet along the floor. Noah and Richie moved in behind her, each boy peering over one of her shoulders. The frogs began to hop. They sprang forward off their back legs and slid down the glass aquarium wall, exposing their bright pink underbellies and twiggy, outstretched legs. Their white eyes, like round Christmas tree bulbs, were locked on the scouts.

"I don't believe this," Noah said. But deep inside, he did believe this. In fact, after everything he'd been through, he almost expected this.

"They see us," Richie said.

"No," Ella said. "They *know* us."

Ella was right. The animals—from Marlo to Mr. Tall Tail to Blizzard to the pink frogs trapped in this tank—recognized Noah, Ella, and Richie. Noah didn't understand why or how, but he was certain that it had something to do with Megan.

Ella reached out and touched the glass. The frogs leaped toward her fingertips. They seemed drawn to her hand the way scraps of steel are drawn to a magnet. She slid her fingertips along the glass, and the frogs hopped toward them, climbing, rolling, and springing off one another.

"No way," Noah said.

The scene reminded him of a plasma ball—an extraordinary clear ball in which threads of lightning streaked toward the glass the second your fingertips touched the surface. Ella seemed to control the frogs just as a person could control those tiny strands of lightning.

She yanked her hand off the glass and backed away.

"What?" Richie asked. "What's wrong?"

"We'd better not draw any attention to ourselves," Ella warned.

"You're right," Noah said. "We don't need any attention—especially from creepy zoo workers."

Richie nodded, and they walked deeper into the exhibit. A few minutes later, Ella pointed to a small room. It protruded out into the space of the hall, its one side flush with the wall of aquariums. The room had a single purpose: to provide a dark viewing area for the aquarium along its wall. The room looked out of place juxtaposed with the aquariums set in the walls.

"There!" she said. "That's the Chamber of Lights."

Richie and Noah nodded; the scouts knew the exhibit from previous visits. They turned, walked a third of the way down the hall, and stopped abruptly. Their eyes swelled. Richie's lips quivered. All the animals were staring at them from the tanks on either side. Snakes slithered near the fronts of their enclosures, their flickering tongues lapping the air. Tree frogs balanced on branches, their still, bulbous eyes fixed outward. Fish idled along the front boundary of their tanks, their sides turned as each stared out with one eye. Lizards leaned against the glass, their gazes pointed at the scouts.

"C'mon," Noah said. "Ignore it. Just keep moving."

They rushed down the hall. Even without looking at the animals, Noah knew that a hundred beady eyes were fixed on him and his friends. He could feel them.

They reached the Chamber of Lights. A black velvet curtain with gold rings hung over its entrance.

"Let's check it out," Noah said.

Ella took a deep breath, and Richie shook the nervousness out of his body. Together the scouts pushed the curtain aside and entered the small room. An aquarium was set inside the wall facing the entrance. The room was small—the size of a large closet. Richie closed the curtain behind them, and the room was enveloped in darkness. The flashlight fish started to blink, and Noah was reminded of a magical night sky filled with winking stars.

He tried to move around and realized how utterly dark the room was.

"Richie," he said, "open the curtain."

Richie threw back the curtain, and the darkness huddled in a long shadow on the far side of the room.

"Look around," Noah said. "See if you see anything."

The walls and ceiling were draped in more black velvet fabric. Other than that, the room was simple, and there was nothing unusual about the tank.

"I don't see anything," Ella said.

Noah slid his palms along the walls. "Something in here grabbed Megan's attention," he said.

"But what?" Richie asked. "Nothing is in here but fish."

"Wait a minute," Ella said. The expression on her face changed several times as she rummaged through her thoughts. "I wonder if we're looking in the wrong place."

"What?" Noah asked. "Megan specifically said—"

"Maybe she saw whatever she saw from outside this place," Ella said.

Noah and Richie were quiet as they tried to grasp what she was getting at.

"C'mon," Ella said. "Follow me."

And that was exactly what Noah and Richie did.

CHAPTER 9

SECRETS OF THE
CHAMBER OF LIGHTS

"Here comes one now!"

Noah had spotted a security guard strolling down the corridor. It was the same one he'd seen at the langur exhibit—the one with red hair and fat lips. He held a set of keys tied to a long string, and as he walked, he swung them in a big circle.

"This is the guy who talked to me when I met Mr. Tall Tail. He's weird."

"Keep your eye on him," Ella said.

The scouts were sitting on a bench in a theater that was less than thirty feet from the Chamber of Lights. The theater was a small room with fifteen seats packed tightly together. The entrance to the theater was from the hallway leading to the Chamber of Lights. The wall that the room shared with the hallway was barely a wall; only four feet high, it merely sectioned off the room. In the front of the theater was a big television that played the same ten-minute video again and again. On the screen, a pair of cartoon frogs kept explaining how ". . . some tree frogs are . . . *rrr-ribit*! . . . poisonous, and *vvveeerrryyy* . . . *rrr-ribit*! . . . deadly." The Action Scouts weren't interested in poisonous tree frogs. They were sitting in the tiny theater because it kept them out of sight while offering a clear view of the Chamber of Lights.

"What do you think he's gonna do?" said Richie.

"I don't know," Ella said. "Just watch."

The worker patrolled the length of the hall and turned back without glancing at the Chamber of Lights. He ambled past the theater and disappeared.

"Well," Richie whispered, "he didn't even look at the chamber."

"Just hold on," Ella said as she checked her watch. "The zoo doesn't close for almost an hour, and we know how weird things get at closing time."

The scouts waited. Hiding behind the short wall, they spied on people moving up and down the hallway. They waited. They watched. They listened to the goofy cartoon frogs spout on and on about the "different . . . *rrr-ribit*! . . . kinds of frogs." At one point, a child entered the theater, took a seat, and hurried off quickly after growing bored with the video. A little later, a lady's voice projected through a loudspeaker. She announced in a rushed voice that the zoo would be closing in ten minutes, ". . . so please make your way to the exits, thank you very much, have a nice day, please drive safely." Creepy Critters promptly emptied. The building fell silent except for the soft gurgle of bubbles and the occasional reptilian croak or hiss or rattle.

"We'd better go," Richie said, "before the zoo closes and we get locked in."

"No!" Ella said, disagreeing. "We stay."

"We what?"

"I have this feeling that we need to be here when the zoo's closed and the employees think everyone's gone."

"That's crazy!" Richie said. "Stay *past* closing time? We could get in serious trouble, and I don't want—"

"She's right," Noah said. "We'll hide here for an hour. If nothing happens, we'll sneak out. It can't be too hard to get out of the zoo, right?"

"Are you guys nuts? Our parents will be home by then! Have you lost your—"

"Richie," Noah said, "it might mean finding my sister."

Richie considered this. "Okay," he said at last. "We stay."

The three children sat in silence. A half hour passed. Nothing happened. Richie was about to say something when Ella stuck out her hand and pinched his lips shut with her fingers.

"Shh! Quiet!" She leaned her ear toward the corridor. "Someone's coming!"

The scouts heard a strange shuffling sound down the hallway. Peering over the short theater wall, they couldn't see who—or what—was approaching. It made scratching sounds against the floor. *Sssheeettt! Sssheeettt! Sssheeettt!* The children rolled off the bench and huddled on the carpet.

Noah whispered, "Are we hiding because we're afraid or because we hope we won't get caught?"

"I don't know," Ella answered. "Both, I guess."

Sssheeettt! Sssheeettt!

They crouched and peered over the wall. A moment later, they discovered the source of the sound: a zoo worker with more hair on his face than his head. He was strolling down the corridor, pausing occasionally to tap on the tanks playfully.

"Hello, Justice," he said to a creature inside a tank. "Good evening, Starlight," he said to another. "Glad to see you both back tonight."

"Back?" Noah whispered. "Back from where?"

The worker casually looked toward the theater, and

the scouts dropped like turtles ducking into their shells. They waited. When the sound of his footsteps faded, they poked their heads up again and stared down the hallway.

"What's he doing?" Richie asked.

"I don't know," Noah said. "Just standing next to the Chamber of Lights."

"He's getting ready," Ella said firmly.

"Getting ready for what?" Richie said.

The man checked over his shoulder and slipped into the Chamber of Lights. He put on a pair of sunglasses and flung the curtain closed.

"Sunglasses?" Noah asked. "For what?"

"I have this feeling we should get down," Ella said.

Noah was about to ask why when a soundless flash of light—as sudden as a camera flash and a hundred times more powerful—sprayed out from the gaps in the curtain covering the entrance to the Chamber of Lights. The scouts fell backward and covered their faces. After a few seconds, they sat up.

Rubbing his eyes, Noah said, "What happened?"

Ella stepped out of the theater and headed toward the chamber.

"Ella!" Richie screamed under his breath. "Don't be stupid!"

Richie and Noah ran after her.

"Ella—*don't*!" Richie warned again.

But Ella would not be persuaded. She marched to the Chamber of Lights, threw back the curtain, and walked inside. Terrified, Richie and Noah stopped in their tracks and held their breath. Noah glanced at Richie—his friend was so helplessly frozen in place that he looked like a strange, misplaced lawn ornament. A moment later, Ella strolled out, and the boys sighed with relief.

"He's gone," she stated.

"But how?" Noah asked.

"It's as if all that light evaporated him," Richie whispered. "Or took him away."

"Away where?"

"I don't know. Someplace else."

Behind them, an angry voice cut the air. "What the heck!"

They spun around. Walking down the hall was the gangly security guard with red hair and fat lips.

"You kids need to beat it," the guard yelled as he marched up to them. "And I mean NOW!"

His breath gushed with the last word, and Noah could smell what he'd eaten for lunch—something with enough garlic to gag a dinosaur. The scouts were too scared to say anything. Whoever this man was, he'd just seen what had happened, and that made him a part of whatever was going on.

"Uh . . . sure, mister," Noah blurted.

"C'mon!" the guard barked. The scouts couldn't move. The worker leaned toward them and yelled, "I said MOOOVE!" He sounded like a cow and even looked like one with his big lips quivering.

The scouts hurried up the hallway. The guard marched behind them, swinging his keys in a circle. Now the swing seemed menacing.

"What's best at this point," he said calmly, "is for you kids to forget what you just saw. Remembering is only gonna do a lot of people a whole lot of harm—and you don't wanna be responsible for that now, do ya?"

As the children walked along the corridor, Noah noticed that the creatures in the aquariums were watching them. In the front of the tanks, fish darted restlessly in the water, snakes slithered anxiously, and frogs jumped in all directions. Then they started to croak, hiss, and snort. The noises built up until the exhibit sounded like an overactive swamp.

"Don't worry about those creatures," the redheaded guard said, raising his voice to be heard over the animal sounds.

"Mister?" Noah said.

"Shut up, kid!"

"How do the animals know who we are?"

"Shut up—and I mean it!" The man's spit sprayed Noah's neck. "You kids have no idea what you're getting into! This is none of your business!"

Noah suddenly felt certain that the man behind him knew something about Megan and her disappearance. From the peculiar guard at the Polar Pool, to Megan's distrust of the zoo workers, to the behavior of the animals, to the guard who had just disappeared in the Chamber of Lights, too much implicated the zoo and its staff with the disappearance of his sister.

Noah exploded with anger. He spun around and shouted, "Where's Megan?"

"Where's *who*?"

"My sister! You know *exactly* who she is, and you know *exactly* how I can find her!" He became more furious with every word. "Take me to her! Take me to her right NOW!"

The guard's face turned white, probably more from shock than anything else. He grabbed a fistful of Noah's shirt and hissed, "Listen, brat! It's time for you and your—"

"Let me go!" Noah struggled to break free but only managed to entangle himself in his own shirt. "Let me go, I said!"

"Let go of him, you big jerk!" Ella yelled. She kicked the guard in the shin.

"Ooowww! Stupid kids!" With his free hand, the guard snatched a walkie-talkie off his hip. "Tank! Come in! Tank! I got a code red on the Megan Situation in Creepy Critters! Requesting backup!"

"The Megan Situation?" Noah said. "You have a *name* for it?"

"Quiet, kid!"

"Let . . . GO!" Noah shrieked.

Ella booted the man in the ankle, and Richie grabbed hold of his shirt.

"Ooowww! Stinkin' brats!"

Creepy Critters' double doors burst open. Standing just outside was a large, beefy man. When he walked through the door frame, he filled it completely. His hands were as large as oven mitts, and his head was so bald and shiny that it glowed. His brown skin was deep and rich and oddly perfect—without a single blemish.

"Tank!" the redheaded guard called out. "Give me a hand with this slippery punk!"

Tank trudged down the corridor and stopped in front of Noah. He crossed his massive arms over his massive body, nearly splitting the seams of his shirt. He was gigantic—the biggest man Noah had ever seen.

"Funny," Noah panted as he struggled to get loose. "You certainly don't look like—let me go!—any security guard I've ever seen . . . around here!"

"Quit squirming, kid," the redheaded guard barked.

"Time to go, little man," said Tank in a deep, throaty voice.

"Where's my sister?"

"She's gone, kid," the guard said. He released Noah and added, "You're just gonna have to get used to that. Tank, get this pesky Action Scout outta my face!"

"Hey!" Ella cried. "How do you know who we are?"

"Kid," the guard said, *"everyone* knows who you are."

"What? Wait! What's going on?"

"Where's my sister!" Noah yelled. "I wanna—"

But before he could finish his sentence, Tank scooped him up and slung him over his shoulder like a beach towel.

"Let him down!" Ella demanded.

She tried to pack a punch, but Tank reached out his enormous arm, seized her wrist, and proceeded to drag her behind him. He hauled his two captives out of the exhibit and down a path that led to a private exit behind the otter exhibit. Richie chased after them. When Tank reached the gates, he kicked one open and dropped Noah on the ground like a sack of laundry. Then, with a clean jerk of his arm, he flung Ella on top of Noah.

Richie squatted beside his friends and yelled, "Hey! You can't do that!"

"Quiet!" Tank bellowed.

"I'm gonna report—"

"QUIET!" The booming thunder of the man's voice made the scouts pull back as if they were dodging a punch.

Tank lowered his voice to a whisper. "Is Charlie Red still behind me?"

"Who?" Ella asked.

"Charlie Red. The other guard."

Confused, Ella said, "N-n-no."

"Good. Listen! I gotta make this quick." He glanced over his shoulder and added, "It looks like you kids are in this now. If the rumors are true, I guess we have Marlo and Blizzard and Mr. Tall Tail to thank for that."

"What are you talking about?" said Ella.

"Be quiet and listen. Megan's Inside. She's in trouble. Some of us on the Inside want to help. Some are too afraid of—" Tank looked around nervously. "I shouldn't even be saying this. He could be anywhere. He lives in the shadows. Heck, he *is* the shadows."

"Who?" Noah said. "Who are you talking about?"

"No time for questions. This has gotta be crazy for you guys, but there's too much to explain. I'll just say this: Do not draw attention to yourselves the way you did today! That was a big mistake. The more people that know about this, the more dangerous things will get."

"Know about what?" Richie asked. "Who's in danger?"

"Everyone," Tank said. "The whole world."

"What? You're not making any sense!" Ella said.

"That's it. I can't talk anymore. Charlie's watching, and he . . . well, he ain't rooting for you, if you know what I'm saying." Tank stepped backward. "Tell nobody. And I mean *nobody*! We'll work through this, I promise you.

I'll see that you guys make it to the Inside."

"The inside of what?" Noah demanded.

"The *Inside*." Tank paused as if he was considering something. He turned to walk off and suddenly swung back around. "Listen, they're really gonna try to stop you now, so we need to speed this up. Noah, I need you to do something for me."

"What? How do you know my name? How do—"

"Check your mailbox."

"My mailbox? Tomorrow?"

"No. Tonight. At midnight. Exactly midnight. Not a second later."

"Wha—?"

"No more questions," Tank said. "Let's just say I suddenly had an idea."

"Wait!" Noah said.

"Gotta go. Remember, beware of the shadows. They listen and they see. And keep this quiet. I promise it will make sense soon. Come back when . . . well . . ." Tank smiled and winked. "Come back when you can stay awhile."

"Tank! Hold on!" Noah called out. "I don't understand!"

But Tank slammed the gate shut and bolted it. The scouts watched in silence as he ran back into the zoo. In a matter of seconds, he disappeared deep into its mystery and magic.

❧ CHAPTER 10 ❧

MIDNIGHT MAIL

Noah sat on the edge of his bed in his dark room and stared at the clock: 11:53. On their walk home from the incident at Creepy Critters earlier that day, the scouts had decided that Noah should check his mailbox as instructed and then report to Ella and Richie first thing in the morning. Now Noah's parents were asleep, and he was ready to move.

11:54. Noah expected to find something in the mail-box, but he didn't know what. Though he hadn't figured out much, he was certain about one thing: anything was possible.

11:55. It was time. He sneaked downstairs, put on a jacket, and slipped out into the cold, dark night. The sky was starless. As he headed for the mailbox, he threw his hood up and stuffed his hands into his pockets.

"It's c-c-cold," he mumbled. His breath rose like steam in front of him.

As he walked down the driveway, he checked his watch. It was 11:56. He opened the mailbox but saw nothing inside except a dry leaf.

"Maybe I'm early."

He glanced at his watch just as 11:57 turned to 11:58.

He rocked back and forth to stay warm. The neighborhood was so quiet that he could hear the wind rustling the few dry leaves that still hung on the trees.

11:58. Noah waited . . . and waited. 11:58 morphed into 11:59. Then 12:00—midnight! Nothing happened. The time on his watch changed to 12:01 . . . 12:02 . . . 12:03.

"Maybe my watch is fast," he mumbled. "Maybe—"

He heard a low sound and peered down the street. He could see nothing but darkness.

"I'm hearing things," he told himself. "I'm just—"

He heard the sound again and fell silent. This time, he was certain that it was something, but what, he didn't know. It was soft, like feet tapping the pavement in the distance.

"Hello?" he said.

A form began to take shape in the distance. Something was running toward him. Noah took a step back and bumped into the mailbox. The clank of the metal box made him yelp.

"Don't panic," he told himself. "You were expecting something like this."

But he wasn't sure what he'd expected. He had no idea what was out there. Tank had seemed to be on his side when he spoke to the scouts outside the zoo gates, but how did he know Tank wouldn't double-cross him? Maybe Tank was Charlie Red's best friend. Maybe the two zoo workers wanted to get rid of Noah and keep the Megan Situation a secret.

The tapping grew louder, and Noah started to make out the form down the road. Whatever the creature was, it was running on four legs. Noah didn't know what to do. He'd never been so confused in his life.

"It must be a dog," he said hopefully.

But he knew better. The thing running toward him was no dog. It was something that had escaped from the zoo. It was something that was following Tank's orders to meet Noah at this hour, at this specific spot. It was something that could be friend or enemy—just like Tank.

Noah's stomach leaped up to his chest. Maybe this was how they'd kidnapped his sister. Maybe they'd tricked her.

"Run, Noah!" he told himself. "Run back to the house *now*."

But he couldn't run, and he wouldn't hide—not with so many unanswered questions. Not with Megan still missing! He felt sick. He felt betrayed.

At that moment, in the cold and darkness, he closed his eyes and allowed the unknown animal to bear down on him.

CHAPTER 11

AT ELLA'S HOUSE

Ella lay in bed, unable to sleep. She was thinking about Blizzard, Tank, Charlie Red, the Chamber of Lights, and the rest of the craziness. She had no idea what Noah would find in his mailbox tonight.

She rolled out of bed, put on her slippers, and walked downstairs. She poured a glass of water and flopped onto the couch. Something was bothering her, but she didn't know what. She grabbed the TV remote and propped her feet up on the coffee table. Her slippers were pink and furry, and they looked like two pink Chihuahuas begging for a snack. She surfed the channels.

Ella tried to pinpoint what was bugging her. The clock above the television said it was midnight. Right now, Noah would be checking his mailbox.

A man on the TV was sitting in a diner, puffing a cigarette. Across from him was another man. The man with the cigarette passed a wad of cash across the table, and in an instant, a team of police officers burst into the room and handcuffed him. What had happened was obvious: the man smoking the cigarette had been framed.

The remote slipped from Ella's fingers and crashed to the floor. She suddenly knew what was bothering her.

"Noah . . ." she muttered. "He's being set up."

She sprang from the sofa and stood in the middle of the living room, not sure what to do.

"Now wait a minute," she whispered. "That guy—Tank—he's on our team."

Was that true? How could she know? She couldn't. That was the problem. Ella ran for the door, grabbed her jacket and earmuffs, and bolted outside, not bothering to change out of her slippers. She raced across her lawn and headed for Noah's house.

❧ CHAPTER 12 ☙

THE SPOTTED MESSENGER

Noah stood beside his mailbox and watched the animal close in on him, a silhouette against the deeper black of night. It wore the darkness like a cloak. Noah could make out the way it resembled a dog, only taller and leaner. Its legs were blurs along its sides. The thing rounded a turn in the street, its paws drumming the pavement, and streaked through a spray of porch light. For a second Noah saw the primary markings on its fur.

Spots.

It ran past the Mathurases' house, trotted past the Smiths' bungalow, and within seconds was less than five houses away. The night seemed to melt off its body as it slowly became visible. Noah saw its pointed ears, its white chin, its short snout, its coal-black nose. Then he saw the details in the animal's markings: black lines and black dots and an overall color that appeared to be orange. The animal abruptly came to a near stop less than ten feet away from Noah. As it prowled the remaining distance, Noah swung around his mailbox for protection. He couldn't believe what he was seeing. A cheetah! As crazy as it seemed, a wildcat from the zoo was loose in Noah's neighborhood.

Noah was so nervous that he made a joke. "You're late, you know."

The cheetah advanced carefully and deliberately, stopped in front of Noah, and rolled its head from side to side. Noah saw its coarse white whiskers and marks that fell like tears from the corners of its eyes. In its mouth was a small woven pouch.

"What's that?"

The animal dropped the pouch and stared at Noah. It tipped its head to one side, growled softly, and nudged the pouch forward with the tip of its nose.

"What's inside?" Noah asked.

The cheetah gave Noah a final look. It whisked around in a flash and raced back down the street, swinging its long tail. In a matter of seconds, it had disappeared into the night.

Noah looked down at the pouch. He didn't want to open it.

"Oh boy," he muttered. "This is crazy. I've got to tell Mom and Dad or somebody."

But then he remembered Tank's warning: "Tell nobody. . . . The more people that know about this, the more dangerous it could get."

Then again, was Tank really on his side? Noah snagged the pouch off the lawn and opened it. Something fell out and clinked on the pavement. A gold key!

"What—?"

Inside was a note. Noah pulled it out and squinted at the page. He couldn't see the words. He charged up his driveway and opened his mother's car door, activating the dome light. Noah fell into the passenger seat and read the note.

> *Noah,*
>
> *Here's the key to the zoo. It works on every door. Use it. Once you get inside, get your butt to Penguin Palace. A penguin named Podgy is waiting for you. He's the biggest penguin in the palace, so you won't have any trouble recognizing him. Like Marlo and Blizzard, he wants to help.*
>
> *Be careful. A lot of people aren't gonna be*

too excited to see you. In fact, there are some
who'd do anything to stop you and the other
Action Scouts from finding Megan.

C-ya on the Inside,
Tank

Noah looked across his backyard toward what was now the cold and ominous wall of the zoo.

"Tank," he muttered, "whose side are you on?"

Noah wondered again if he was being led into a trap. Tank had told them that the fate of the world rested on keeping the zoo's secrets safe. How far would Tank go to ensure this? There was only one way to find out.

"I can't wait for morning. I can't wait for Ella and Richie. This needs to be done now."

Noah dropped the key in his pocket, darted into the garage, and dragged out his dirt bike. Halfway down the driveway, he hopped on the seat and sped off. He raced into the wind, the cold air stinging his skin.

"I'm on my way, Megan," he said. "Hold tight."

As he drove along the road, he noticed something in the Parkers' yard. Beside a big pine tree, someone or something was moving. Noah looked closer until he realized whatever had been there was gone. Nothing remained but the shadows.

❧ CHAPTER 13 ❧
ELLA ON THE RUN

Ella cut through her neighbors' yards on her way to Noah's house. She hurdled the hedges in Mrs. Ryan's yard and dodged the lawn ornaments at Mrs. Pierre's. She jumped fences and ducked tree limbs. Once a branch snagged her earmuffs, and she had to turn around to snatch them back. As she neared Noah's house, she saw someone in the driveway. It was Noah. He was climbing onto his bike.

"Noah!" she called out. "Noah, wait!"

But Noah sped out of sight before she could get his attention.

Ella ran into Noah's yard and happened to kick something on the lawn beside the mailbox. She picked it up. A pouch. She poked her fingers inside and found it empty.

"Something was in here," she said. "Something important."

She spun around and took off to find Richie, who lived on her street. She went back home the same way she'd come, but this time, when she cut across Mrs. Pierre's lawn, she crashed into a pink flamingo and flattened it to the ground.

At Richie's house, she found a spot beneath his second-story bedroom window and pulled a small clump of dirt from a flower bed. She pitched it at the glass. She waited a few seconds and then hurled another handful of dirt at the window.

"C'mon, Richie!" she whispered frantically. "Wake up!"

Suddenly she gasped. From the corner of her eye, she'd caught sight of someone standing in the next yard. A man. Tall and lean, he wore a hat with a wide, circular brim. He had broad shoulders and a long dark trench coat. Standing with his hands clasped behind his back, he was watching Ella, watching her from the shadows. So deep and dark were the shadows that they hid his face, his eyes, and his intentions.

Then he vanished. But not in the all-at-once way that

an imaginary thing disappears. Rather, he dissolved. It was as if he'd melted into the shadows.

Ella felt goose bumps crawl over her skin. She tried to tell herself that the man hadn't been there at all and that her overworked mind was playing tricks on her. But what had Tank said? Beware of the man who "lives in the shadows . . . he *is* the shadows."

A fresh round of goose bumps dotted her arms, and she tried to rub them away. She glanced up at Richie's window. It was finally sliding open.

❧ CHAPTER 14 ❧

AT RICHIE'S HOUSE

ichie sat up in bed and listened. Seconds later, he heard it again—a soft *thump*! against his window. He jumped out of bed, flicked on the lights, and opened the window. Someone was standing in his yard.

"Richie!"

"Who's out there?"

"Richie, it's me!"

"Ella?"

"We've got a big problem! It's Noah! I think he's going in!"

"Into the zoo?"

"No, the *bathroom*." She tossed up one more clump of earth. It missed Richie but sailed through the window and landed in the middle of his pillow. "Of course, the zoo!"

"When?"

"Right now!"

Richie thought about this for a moment. Then he said, "What are we gonna do?"

"The only thing we can do," Ella said. "Go in after him."

"Seriously?"

"Dead serious!" Ella slid backward, saying, "Meet me in my front yard! Give me two minutes so I can get dressed!"

Richie didn't move. He stood in silence, stunned.

"Richie?"

He took a breath. "Two minutes," he said at last. "Gotchya."

Ella took off across the lawns. Her open jacket trailed behind her like a short cape. Richie remained still for another moment.

"I can't believe this is happening," he muttered.

He started to close the window and stopped. Something was moving on the lawn next door. Richie peered into the darkness, but he saw nothing.

"Hello?" he called out of the window.

The wind murmured, but that was it.

"Who's there?"

No answer.

He was certain that he'd seen something. A man. A man with a strange hat.

"Forget it," he said at last.

He closed the window, jumped into his clothes, and prepared for the next event—whatever that might turn out to be.

CHAPTER 15
THE KEY

Fifty feet from the zoo gate, Noah stopped pedaling. He coasted silently to the entrance, dismounted, and ducked behind the bushes. Beside the gate was a glass booth. Inside, a light and a small TV were on, but the guard wasn't there. Noah crouched down and ran toward the gate, pulling his bike beside him.

He plucked the gold key out of his pocket and poked it in the slot. It didn't fit. He turned it over and tried again. No luck.

"C'mon, you stupid thing."

He heard a cough. Inside, a guard was coming toward

him. Noah tried to force the key in. Even the tip didn't fit.

"C'mon, c'mon, c'mon!" he muttered. "Don't do this!"

Another cough—this time, much closer. Noah heard the man's feet shuffling.

"Fit, you stupid—"

Then something magical happened. The key transformed. Its ridges melted, and its bumpy edge became smooth. Noah stared at the flat key in his hand, confused.

"Wha—?"

Noah could hear the guard's footsteps. He was closing on Noah, reaching the end of a path that ran between a pair of long hedges. In a panic, Noah stabbed the key at the slot. This time, it slipped in and the lock opened with a soft click. When he pulled the key out, the sharp ridges were back.

"No way!" he mumbled.

Seconds before the guard rounded the hedge, Noah grabbed his bike, slipped through the gate, and coasted into the shadows.

He was inside. At least part of the way.

CHAPTER 16

ELLA AND RICHIE
HAVE A GREAT FALL

"Let me get this straight," Richie said. He and Ella were standing beside an oak tree near the zoo wall in their neighbor's backyard. They were looking at a branch that ran across the top of the wall. "That branch is at least twenty feet high. You want to climb up there, walk across it, leap onto the wall, and then jump into the zoo?"

"Good plan, don't ya think?"

"I guess that depends on what kinds of animals are in there."

"Probably a bunch of peacocks," Ella assured him. She suddenly noticed something about Richie. He was wearing leather boots instead of his normal running shoes. "Where the heck are your shoes?"

"In here," Richie said as he adjusted a backpack he'd brought with him. "Along with some other stuff. Supplies, you know."

"How come you're not wearing 'em?"

"They're kinda flashy."

"Good point," Ella said with an understanding nod. "Probably not a good idea to bust into the zoo with shoes that practically glow in the dark."

Richie pointed to the tree and shifted the conversation back to a greater concern. "You think that branch will hold us?"

Ella tipped her head and considered his query for a moment. Her answer came out like a question: "Yes?"

"That's convincing."

"C'mon, Richie! Don't go and wimp out on me."

"We shouldn't even be in this yard," Richie said. "We're trespassing."

"Yeah," Ella said. "But since we're about to sneak into the zoo in the middle of the night, I don't think standing in someone's grass is such a big deal."

Richie couldn't think of an answer to that.

"Listen, Richie. We don't have a choice. I mean, we've already lost Megan to whatever's going on in that crazy zoo. Are we ready to lose Noah, too?"

"Okay," Richie said. "You're right."

Ella nodded and sprang into action. With the grace of a gymnast, she jumped, twirled, kicked, and heaved her way up the tree. Within seconds, she reached the branch twenty feet in the air.

With some effort, a little time to recoup halfway, and a lot of grunting and whimpering, Richie managed to make his way up. Ella nodded at him and headed out across the branch, which ran parallel to the ground. She used smaller branches that stemmed from it for support and moved easily from one point to the next, stepping over patches of twigs and leaves. In no time, she swung down to the concrete wall, which had a wide, flat cap that overhung both sides by a few inches.

"See any animals?" Richie called out.

Ella gazed over the wall. "Nunh-unh. It's too dark. You've got your penlight, right?"

Richie patted his chest pocket. "Just like a good scout."

"Okay. Your turn."

Richie inspected the distance beneath him. "Here I come . . . I guess," he said.

He took his first step, slipped, and started to flap his arms to keep his balance. His hips shifted from side to side, and his rear end pushed out in different directions.

"Richie, be careful!"

He managed to grab a branch and steady himself. After

taking a few minutes to find his composure, he wiped his sweaty forehead and started again. He eventually traversed the branch and jumped down to the wall. He pulled out his penlight.

"Let's see what's down there," Ella said.

Richie tried to flick the switch of his penlight and instead flicked it right out of his hand! It clanked down on the wall, bounced once, and disappeared into the darkness of the zoo. The children stared down in disbelief.

"Oops," Richie said.

"Forget about it," Ella said. "We'll take our chances."

"Are you sure? There could be more than peacocks down there."

"Let's hope not."

They sat down on the wall and prepared to jump.

"You ready?" Ella asked.

"I'm ready."

"On three?"

"On three."

"Okay! Here we go." Ella licked her top lip and started the count. "One . . . two . . . THREE!"

They pushed off the wall and plunged into the shadows. They free-fell for what seemed to Ella a very long time, but was probably just a second or two. When Ella hit the ground, bolts of pain shot through her knees. The scouts had landed on a hill, and immediately they started to roll. Ten somersaults later, they came to a stop. Unfortunately it happened to be in a pool of thick mud. Even more unfortunately, something beside Ella was breathing in her face, grunting an angry animal grunt.

It was no peacock.

❦ CHAPTER 17 ❧

THE WAY TO PENGUIN PALACE

Noah rode quietly across the zoo along the maze of winding paths. Light fell from overhead lamps and the eaves of the zoo buildings, cutting cone-shaped wedges out of the darkness—wedges that Noah dodged in order to stay hidden.

After speeding past Giraffic Jam, he turned onto a dirt path surrounded by trees. The area was marked as a nature preserve. His bike splashed through puddles and clunked across two bridges made of wooden planks. At the end of the path, Noah bounced back onto the side-walk. He raced past the A-Lotta-Hippopotami exhibit, rolled through Arctic Town, and sped around Creepy Critters.

He neared Metr-APE-olis and spotted two distant figures strolling toward him. He got off his bike and ducked behind the bushes. When the leaves stopped rustling, he realized that the faraway voices belonged to men. As they approached, their voices grew louder. Finally Noah could make out the words.

"Then Tank showed up and got rid of 'em," one man said.

"He didn't hurt them, did he?" This fellow had an annoying, squeaky voice. It reminded Noah of a dog's chew toy.

"Not that I know. I heard he just got rid of 'em."

Noah realized they were talking about the scouts.

"They'll be back, I suppose."

"Let's just hope they don't get the police involved," the other man squeaked.

"For pete's sake, Henry! Don't even mention such a thing!"

As they passed Noah, their conversation changed to another subject. They kept walking, their footsteps softened, and their voices faded away.

Noah sat for a moment and tried to sort through his feelings. Finally he said to himself, "Tank, why don't I trust you?" He considered this and realized his feelings didn't matter anymore. It was too late to turn back. With that, he hopped onto his bike and tore down the path.

He pedaled past Metr-APE-olis, coasted by the Forest of Flight, rolled to a stop at Penguin Palace, and hid his bike in the bushes. He swiped his key out of his pocket and held it up to the lock. The key worked its magic. When he turned his wrist—*click!*—the lock opened. The hinges squeaked as Noah pushed the door open with his shoulder. Before him was the dark interior of Penguin Palace.

"I'm getting close, Megan."

He took a deep breath and stepped inside, ready for anything. Or so he thought.

CHAPTER 18

ELLA HOLDS HER BREATH

Ella didn't dare move. Mud oozed between her fingers and seeped into her pants and shoes. It was too dark to see the animal, but she could hear its gravelly grunts and feel the heat rising from its skin. It sloshed through the mud, shifting the earth beneath her. Then it snorted, and a burst of snot pushed her head aside.

Ella was sitting up. She could faintly see movement to her left. Richie! He was writhing in the mud, mumbling something.

"Richie, stay still," Ella whispered. "Don't move."

The animal grunted, and as it moved closer, the ground

trembled. A wave of mud splashed across Ella's lap.

"Ella?"

"Shh!"

The animal nudged her shoulder. Its touch was hard, smooth, and sharp. A cold edge slid against her cheek and knocked her earmuffs askew. The animal backed a few steps away, and a new round of tremors shook the ground. Seconds later, Ella felt the creature push against her spine.

"Ella," Richie said. "It's—it's—"

Richie was trying to tell her what the animal was, but she didn't need that. She'd just figured out that the sharp thing pushing against her was at the end of the animal's snout. And she could think of only one animal that carried such a peculiar feature in such a peculiar spot.

"It's a rhino!" Richie finished.

As he said the word, the beast moved its deadly horn to the base of Ella's spine. She held her breath and hoped she wouldn't feel too much pain.

CHAPTER 19

A Palace Built for Penguins

Noah stepped into Penguin Palace and closed the door softly behind him. The air inside was cold and damp. He entered the main room, which housed a gigantic four-sided aquarium full of penguins.

The aquarium had a view from every side. It reached all the way to the ceiling, covered most of the floor, and was nearly half the size of Noah's school gymnasium. In the middle of the aquarium was a landmass covered with ice. It nearly filled the aquarium. On all sides, the land ended just feet from the glass walls, creating a narrow channel. Full of water, this channel gave the penguins a place to swim. A crowd of penguins was gathered on the icy shore. They were standing around, doing nothing, and looking bored and sad in the strange way that penguins always look bored and sad.

Noah walked up to the glass. One by one, the birds noticed him and waddled to the edge of the ice. They began to rock from side to side and flap their flat flippers. In no time, every penguin had its beady eyes locked on Noah.

"Hello, guys," Noah said. He pressed his palms against the cold aquarium and asked, "Which one of you is Podgy?"

~ CHAPTER 20 ~

LITTLE BIGHORN

The rhino's dagger-sharp curved horn slid up Ella's back, meticulously skipping over each disk in her spine as it slipped beneath her jacket. The enormous animal's simple touch revealed all its might, all its power, and all its potential.

Just when Ella was certain she would be speared, the rhinoceros hoisted her out of the mud with one clean jerk of its head. Ella dangled in the air at the end of its snout.

"Hey!" she said, squirming and kicking the air. "Richie! Help!"

The rhino sloshed through the mud, bouncing and swinging her from its pointed horn like a puppet on a short, fat string. The top band of her earmuffs fell across her face. The animal's every footfall sent a fresh wave of panic over her.

"Put me down!" she grunted.

The rhino started to trot, and she felt the cold wind prick her cheeks. Seconds later, at the end of the yard, the animal swiftly lowered her to the ground.

Ella recovered quickly and spun around. Here, near the zoo lights, she caught her first glimpse of the animal. Its eyes were warm and brown, and in them Ella saw only kindness. The rhino didn't want to harm her—it wanted to help, just the way Blizzard had.

It snorted, spun around, and quaked back into the darkness. Seconds later, she heard Richie shrieking.

"This can't be happening!" Ella shuddered.

The rhino charged out of the shadows, dangling Richie by his backpack. When it reached Ella, it dipped its head and slipped the boy off its spike. Richie scrambled to Ella's side, and together the scouts gazed up at the huge beast.

"It's . . . it's friendly," Richie gasped.

"Maybe they're *all* friendly," Ella said. "At least to us."

She reached up. The rhino lowered its head and allowed Ella to pet the side of its face. Its skin was hard and rough.

"Thanks," Ella said. "For the help, I mean."

The rhino grunted and nudged them toward the main part of the zoo with its massive head.

"It wants us to go," Richie said. "It wants us . . ."

"To find Megan," Ella declared. "Somehow, it knows."

"This is too weird."

"I have a feeling we haven't seen anything yet."

The rhino nudged them again.

"Let's go," Richie said. "I don't wanna be rude to this guy."

"Yeah," Ella said. "Especially when it could make a shish kebab out of us with one poke of its horn."

The rhino nudged them a third time, and the scouts paid heed. They headed off toward a narrow pedestrian bridge that crossed a concrete trench on the perimeter of the rhino exhibit.

"Think we have time to stop Noah?" Richie asked.

"We're not gonna stop him," Ella countered. "We're gonna join him."

"But where is he going?"

"Heck if I know, Richie. Inside—whatever that means."

They crossed the bridge and scrambled to the main path. Ella turned back to look at the sign over the entrance to the exhibit. She'd seen it too many times to count, but reading it now was like reading it for the first time:

WELCOME TO RHINORAMA!

HOME TO THE BIGGEST RHINOCEROS IN NORTH AMERICA

LITTLE BIGHORN

As the scouts raced ahead, Ella whispered, "See you later, Little Bighorn."

Though the words were intended to be a fond farewell, Ella was right: She *would* see Little Bighorn again. She would see a lot of him indeed.

❦ CHAPTER 21 ❧

NOAH HAS COMPANY

Noah walked alongside the glass wall of the aquarium in Penguin Palace. He could only think of one thing—going inside. Inside to the *Inside*. He wasn't sure what that meant or how to do it, but he knew it started with getting into the aquarium.

On the other side of the glass wall, the penguins followed him. Most looked ordinary, but some had messy thickets of orange feathers. Each one waddled along the edge of the icy island, flapping its flippers. They kept bumping into one another, and occasionally one slipped on the ice and splashed into the water.

"If I worked here," Noah said to himself, "how would I get inside this exhibit? How would I—"

Thap! Thap! Thap! Thap!

He sucked back his breath. Someone was on the other side of the aquarium, near the back of the building. By the sound of it, that *someone* was coming toward him.

The penguins crowded the edge of the ice and bobbed in the water.

The person kept making the strange noise. *Thap! Thap! Thap! Thap!* It sounded like a baseball card caught in the spoke of a bicycle wheel. *Thap! Thap! Thap! Thap!* It didn't miss a beat—and it was just around the corner.

Noah was about to turn and run when he saw not a person, but a penguin. The bird was black-and-white and had a yellow patch below his neck. He stood a couple of feet high, and his flippers looked remarkably like long, slender pancakes. He waddled forward as fast as he could go, so his flat feet slapped the concrete—*Thap! Thap! Thap! Thap!* He was headed straight for Noah.

Behind him, a second penguin turned the corner. Then a third, a fourth, a fifth—more and more until a crowd of penguins was rushing toward him. They kept bumping into and falling over one another. Within seconds, Noah was surrounded by the strange birds. He felt the cold rising from their bodies. It was amazing how different they looked outside the aquarium. Their bodies—glossy with ice water—were more colorful and full dimensional. For the first time, the penguins seemed real.

"I need to get inside your aquarium," Noah said. "Can you guys show me how?"

A couple of penguins bumped into his legs, urging him to walk in the direction that they'd come from.

"Okay," Noah said. "Lead the way."

The penguins did exactly that.

ᕙ CHAPTER 22 ᕦ

ELLA BECOMES SPEECHLESS

Ella and Richie sat in a quiet spot outside Metr-APE-olis under a lamppost, trying to figure out where Noah might have gone.

"Arctic Town," Richie said. "All that stuff that happened with Blizzard—I'm sure he picked Arctic Town."

"What about the Forest of Flight?" Ella asked. "Or maybe he went to see that monkey with the long tail."

"I don't know."

"Me neither."

Ella stared up at the sky—a blank canvas for the portrait of her thoughts. For a moment, neither of them spoke.

Then Richie said in a weak voice, "Uh . . . Ella?"

"Not now, Richie. I'm thinking."

"You're gonna want to see this," he insisted.

Ella looked at him. His face was white. His expression was blank, as if he felt no emotion—or as if he felt so many emotions that they canceled one another out like the variables in Mrs. Bluss's mind-bending algebra equations. Ella's eyes followed his gaze, and she gasped with fright.

Finally Richie spoke very quietly. "What . . . are . . . they?"

Ella had no words. Not for this.

❧ CHAPTER 23 ❧

Marching with Penguins

The penguins led Noah to a door in the wall opposite the aquarium. The sign read, EMPLOYEES ONLY. Three penguins jumped at the door and thrust it open.

Inside was a narrow hallway with a steep wooden floor. The penguins led Noah up the ramp. A few feet ahead, the passageway swung around a sharp turn. One penguin lost its balance and rolled down the ramp, knocking over penguins like bowling pins. Looking dazed but no less determined, the fallen penguins jumped to their feet and started their climb again.

The hallway straightened out and headed toward

the aquarium. Moments later, Noah felt cold air rising through the floor; the aquarium was directly beneath them. They reached an open doorway framed with ice. One by one, the penguins leaped through it and dropped out of sight. Noah leaned through the doorway to take a peek and slipped on the snow-covered ramp. He tumbled down and landed flat on the icy shore. The penguins following behind him trampled across his back in single file. Each time Noah tried to yell, "Stop!" a webbed foot landed on his head and pressed his face into the snow.

Finally, when all the penguins had crossed over him, he worked his way to his feet and looked around. The inside of the aquarium was covered in snow, frost, and ice. Penguins were everywhere, and the black eyes of each suited bird were pinned on him.

Noah dusted the snow off his jacket. His breath rose from his mouth like steam. He didn't know what the birds expected from him, so he simply stated his purpose.

"I'm looking for a penguin named Podgy."

CHAPTER 24

AVALANCHE OF FUR

Ella stared in disbelief.

"What are they?" Richie asked again.

Fifty yards away, hundreds of little animals were charging toward them. They covered a long stretch of the sidewalk and spilled onto the grass. Standing just higher than someone's ankles, they were packed so tightly together that they looked like the rushing mass of an avalanche— an avalanche of fur.

"Richie," Ella said slowly, "those things look like rats."

"I was hoping you wouldn't say that," Richie said. "Rats are friendly, right? I mean, that stuff in the movies about rats being mean—they just say that to freak you out, right?"

"I don't know," Ella said. "You're the one with the big brain."

As the animals approached, they grew noisier. Their pin-sized claws scratched the sidewalk and made a high-pitched *cchhiiitt! cchhiiitt!* sound. The animals were barking, but their barks were quiet and squeaky: *Yip! Yip! Yip!*

"Hold on," Ella said. "Those aren't rats. They're gophers."

The closer they came, the easier they were to see. They had short legs; squat, chubby bodies; and heads that looked like furry tennis balls. When they reached the scouts, they surrounded them and sat up on their hind legs, exposing their fat, fuzzy underbellies. They watched Ella and Richie as if they were expecting the children to do something. Now that they were so close, their yipping sounds were louder than ever.

"These are prairie dogs," Richie said. "Not gophers."

Ella leaned toward Richie and said, "Whatever they are, I'm guessing they know who we are."

Richie turned around in circles, eyeing the prairie dogs suspiciously. "I'm guessing you're right."

"You know what else I'm guessing?"

"What?"

"I'm guessing they know Megan. And not only that,

but they know where she is. And that's where Noah's headed."

"If we can't trust Tank," said Richie, "how do you know we can trust these guys?"

"I don't. All I know is we gotta help Noah."

Richie nodded.

Ella looked down at the animals and said, "Okay, fur-balls. Show us what you want to show us."

The mass of prairie dogs turned and headed back in the direction they'd come from, escorting the scouts through the dark, cold night.

CHAPTER 25

NOAH ON ICE

A huge penguin rounded the block of ice. He was as tall as Noah, and he looked like he weighed close to sixty pounds. As he waddled forward, the blubber on his belly rolled from side to side. He stopped in front of the scout, tipped back his head, and casually aimed his bill upward, the way penguins do.

"Podgy?" Noah said. "You are Podgy, right?"

The penguin didn't reply.

"Tank told me to meet you." Noah paused for a second. "Can you understand what I'm saying?"

Still no response.

"Tank said—"

Without warning, the penguin dropped his bill and lunged into Noah. Penguin and boy crashed downward, hit the ice, and rolled into the water. Noah sank. On one side was the icy island; on the other was the long glass wall of the aquarium. He heard muffled splashes, one after another; penguins were diving in around him. They started to swim up and down the channel, churning the water.

Noah panicked and gulped freezing water. His rear end struck something—the bottom of the tank. Looking up, he could see only the white undersides of swimming penguins. He pushed up from the floor of the tank, but a penguin struck him down. Dazed, he sank a second time.

Around him, the icy water churned. He felt faint. He was exhausted. He never should have trusted Tank. Tank had said the fate of the world depended on keeping the secrets of the zoo safe. Noah's life was an easy trade.

Another penguin crashed into him. Noah gulped more water. He knew he was seconds from drowning.

CHAPTER 26

LITTLE DOGS OF THE PRAIRIE

The prairie dogs darted between Ella's legs and across her feet. Every minute or so, one of them yipped so loudly that Ella feared that she'd stepped on it. She checked the bottom of her shoe each time, freaked out by the thought of finding the animal's remains stuck in her treads like a horrible mass of furry gum.

The prairie dogs led the scouts past the zebras and camels to the prairie dog exhibit. Called Little Dogs of the Prairie, it was set in the ground and looked like a long, shallow pool filled with sandy dirt, patches of grass, and tiny mounded hills. The walls along its perimeters were steep and high; they were meant to keep the prairie dogs from getting out. Little Dogs of the Prairie resembled a miniature desert. Across it, the animals had made at least fifty holes—holes that led to a complex maze of underground tunnels.

The animals leaped over the perimeter wall and raced around, raising clouds of dust. Some dived into holes and immediately poked their heads back up to look around; they appeared to Ella to be reassuring themselves that their night operation was progressing smoothly. A few didn't return to the sandy pit; instead, they bit into Ella's and Richie's jeans and pulled them along a narrow sidewalk toward the rear of their habitat.

"Hey!" Ella said.

"My guess," Richie said, as his foot was dragged forward, "is they want us to go *this* way."

Ella knew where they were being taken. At the back of the exhibit, stairs led down to five artificially constructed tunnels, an attraction for young visitors. The tunnels ran beneath the sandy terrain. Children were able to crawl into the tunnels and pop their heads up through special holes on the prairie dog hillsides. Their heads were protected by plastic bubbles that covered the holes and prevented the animals from chewing off their noses. This part of the zoo attraction was affectionately named Little Kids of the Prairie.

The prairie dogs dragged Ella and Richie down the stairs. Then they scattered, leaving the children alone. The scouts dropped to their hands and knees and crawled into the main tunnel. Traces of moonlight illuminated the way.

"Now would be a good time to use that penlight you donated to the rhino exhibit," Ella said.

Richie said nothing; he was familiar with Ella's sharp tongue.

The main tunnel split into five secondary tunnels, which led in different directions. At the end of each one was an open space big enough for a kid to stand up in. Ella crawled along the first tunnel. She stood at the end, poked her head up through the hole, and peered through the plastic bubble. Prairie dogs were scurrying everywhere and diving in and out of holes. One of them saw her and dashed up to the bubble. It pressed its snout against the plastic and yipped once, as if to say hello. Ella yipped once in return, ducked into the tunnel, and crawled back to Richie.

"Did you find anything?" he asked.

"No."

A large prairie dog charged into the tunnel, brushed past them, and headed for another tunnel. At the entrance, he turned around, stood on his hind legs, looked straight at Ella, and yipped repeatedly. Then he ran back, passed them, and fled outside.

"I think he just pointed us to that tunnel," Richie said. "C'mon! Let's check it out."

The scouts crawled along the passageway, and again Ella poked her head up into the plastic bubble at the end.

"Do you see anything?" Richie said. "Anything unusual?"

Ella glanced back and forth. Everything seemed normal.

"No, not at all."

Suddenly a group of prairie dogs on the sandy ground charged at the bubble. They crowded the plastic and blocked almost all the light of the moon. Ella lowered her head and stared at Richie.

"The prairie dogs surrounded the bubble." She shrugged her shoulders. "I don't know what to do."

"Me neither. Look again."

She stood up and poked her head into the little plastic dome. The same crowd of prairie dogs suddenly stood on their hind legs and leaped up to the top of the bubble. Each time an animal jumped, it landed on the plastic surface and slid down the side until its paws were either back on the ground or planted on top of another prairie dog. Ella flinched as she watched the animals strike the bubble and claw it, leaving long, thin scratches on the sides.

"What are they doing?" Richie asked.

"I don't know."

The prairie dogs were yipping so loudly that the bubble couldn't keep out their sounds. Leaping and climbing over one another, they began to cover the bubble from the ground up, their fuzzy undersides pressed against the plastic. They were making themselves into a prairie dog ladder the way cheerleaders make a human pyramid. In less than a minute, the last small prairie dog reached the top of the bubble and fell across the only open spot left on the plastic, covering it completely. The animals stopped climbing, scratching, and yipping. Without the light of the moon and stars, the tunnel was utterly dark. The silence was eerie.

"Richie?"

"Yeah?"

"I don't—"

Crrraaackkk! The plastic bubble shifted. *Crrraaackkk!* All of a sudden, it dropped, and an alarming sound of metal against metal erupted. The walls rumbled, the floor shifted, and large clumps of dirt and sand tumbled down in a torrent. The scouts jumped into each other's arms.

"What's going on?" Richie squealed. "What are they doing?"

"A switch!" Ella said. "The bubble must have fallen against a switch!"

The floor was spinning.

"Ella! What's happening?"

The sound of grinding metal intensified as the whirling floor gained speed. Around and around it went. Ella looked up. The bubble was spinning and flinging prairie dogs into the air.

"Elll-aaa! Whaaa—? Whaaa—? Whaaat's haaappeniiinggg?"

Ella looked down. A circular section of the floor was unthreading like a screw or a soda cap.

"Riiichiiieee!" Ella screamed.

"Whhaaattt?"

"Hooolllddd ooonnn!"

Richie squeezed her tightly. Not a second later, the floor fell out from under them. The scouts plummeted into the unknown reaches of dark earth.

CHAPTER 27

PENGUIN TRAFFIC

Noah knew he couldn't hold his breath a second longer. At that moment, two penguins bit into his jacket collar and dragged him to the surface. He gasped for air and struggled to tread water. His drenched running shoes felt like ten-pound weights strapped to his feet.

Penguins were still diving off the ice. They swam around him, swirling the water with the powerful strokes of their flippers. They looked like wild black-and-white torpedoes with wings.

Terrified, Noah struggled to think of Megan. He imagined her face and her smile. Megan needed him. As penguin-made waves splashed Noah's face, he forced himself to be brave. He was growing colder every moment. He needed to get out of the water, but the bank was too steep. His only hope was to swim around the icy island and find a spot with a more gradual incline.

He took a deep breath and plunged forward, swimming alongside the penguins with a sloppy breaststroke. To his right, he could see through the glass wall of the aquarium into the room that he'd stood in so often. How weird to be inside looking out!

He surfaced for air and swam toward the corner, where there was no glass—only steel and concrete. All the corners had been built this way to support the huge aquarium. They were the only spots that blocked the visitors' view. At each corner, the bottom half of the icy island stopped short of the wall, while the top half stretched completely across the channel, creating a fully submerged tunnel that connected two sides of the square aquarium.

A second before reaching the corner, Noah dunked his head and swam into the shadowy tunnel, kicking and paddling and doing his best to ignore the penguins bumping against him. He turned his body with the turn of the corner and then swam out into the other side of the aquarium, where he thrashed his way to the surface and gasped for air.

It took all of his strength just to tread water. He was

freezing, and the stuffing in his jacket felt like lead. The penguins continued to torpedo around him. One jumped over his head, and another squeezed through his legs.

Swimming in the crowd was Podgy, looking even bigger in the water than on the ground. Floating with his head and back above the surface, he seemed lazy and unconcerned. He circled the boy so closely that his flipper swept against him.

Almost choking, Noah managed to say, "What . . . do you . . . want from me?"

Podgy swam behind Noah, plunged through his legs, and bolted up with Noah situated across his wide back.

"What are you doing?" Noah squealed. He instinctively wrapped his arms around Podgy's fat body and grabbed two handfuls of blubber on the penguin's neck. "I don't . . . trust you! I can't—"

Podgy lurched forward. Noah lay with his stomach flat against the bird's feathered back. As water spilled off his cheeks, the scout wrestled himself into a stable position. The wet penguin was so slippery! All of a sudden, Podgy plunged. Noah barely had time to inhale and hold his breath. In seconds, penguin and boy were speeding through the water several feet below the surface. Noah's legs dangled behind Podgy's rear, and he fought the overwhelming urge just to let go.

They traveled into the tunnel at the second corner

of the aquarium. Darkness enveloped them. A moment later, they burst out on the other side, and Podgy sailed into the air in a graceful arc. Noah took a deep breath before they splashed back down.

Podgy swerved to avoid the slower penguins, and Noah ducked to keep from striking his head against the birds above them. The big penguin swiftly covered the length of the third wall, rounded the next corner, and emerged on the fourth and final side of the aquarium. The penguin porpoised into the air, and again Noah inhaled and held his breath.

This time, Podgy dived to the bottom of the tank. He traveled so close to the floor that Noah's toes skipped off the concrete. The penguins ahead dodged to either side of the aquarium to open a path.

When Podgy and Noah swam into the fourth corner, Podgy jolted and Noah nearly slid off his back. Though it was dark, he could faintly make out a big hole in the side of the ice island, but not an ordinary big hole. It was a cave—a hidden cave! Podgy tucked his flippers against his sides and headed straight toward it. Noah shut his eyes and squeezed the penguin tightly. The two of them slipped inside the cave and left the world that Noah knew behind.

❧ CHAPTER 28 ❧

OUTSIDE INTO THE INSIDE

"*Riiichiiieee!*" Ella barely had time to scream before the floor stopped falling. She was somewhere in the middle of "*iiieee!*" when they hit something with a solid *thump!* The impact sent the two scouts tumbling, and Ella wound up with her face pressed into the ground. She raised her head and spat out a mouthful of sand.

"Richie!" she called out. "You okay?"

Richie lay beside her in a contorted position. He looked as if he were trying to massage his back with his own feet.

"Sort of," he said.

They found themselves in a dirt tunnel that was just wide enough to hold their bodies. Illuminated by overhead lights set in the walls, the tunnel continued straight for about thirty yards and branched at least a dozen times. Some of the branches were on the left; others, on the right. The adjoining crawlways were generally circular, and their diameters varied: one foot, two feet, three feet. They were capable of holding animals of different sizes. The scouts seemed to be in a central tunnel, a place where other, similar passages connected. It ended at what appeared to be a curtain—a velvet curtain with thick folds.

"Uh . . . Ella?" Richie said.

"Yeah?"

"Why is a curtain hanging there . . . in the ground?"

"Beats me," Ella answered.

The ground was crowded with prairie dogs. The skittish animals were running back and forth, diving in and out of the passageways, and acting half crazed as they jumped and bumped into one another. They yipped, squealed, and made an enormous fuss.

A noise erupted behind them, and the scouts peered over their shoulders. The platform that had lowered them into the ground was rising on top of a pole. The pole rotated and threaded the platform back into place, filling the tunnels with dust and cutting them off from the world above.

Richie coughed and muttered, "It's a machine. But how?"

"I don't know," Ella said. "But there's only one way to go now."

The two scouts commenced crawling down the main tunnel, their backs occasionally scraping the low ceiling. Prairie dogs ran beneath them and circled their arms. Ella watched one crash into the rump of a wider prairie dog and then tumble down. It stood up, angrily shook off the dirt, and scampered away.

"Where are they going?" Richie asked.

"I don't know. Back and forth."

"Back and forth to where?"

"I don't know that either. But if we keep crawling, I bet we'll find out."

As they crawled past the mouth of a connecting tunnel, they saw it was covered with a velvet curtain similar to the one ahead of them. Second and third tunnels weren't. Ella didn't understand. And judging by Richie's breathy "Huh?" he didn't either.

They twisted and wriggled through the prairie dogs. One ran beneath Ella, brushing its short, pointy tail across her face. Ella hollered, and the prairie dog yipped, as if to say, "Sorry!" or maybe, "Deal with it!" Then it scurried down the tunnel, wagging its furry fanny.

"These gophers have some nerve," Ella exclaimed.

A prairie dog sprang from a hole and ran across her hands, yipping all the way.

"What am I? Invisible?" she said.

As they neared the curtain, they saw it was red with tassels. It completely covered the passage.

"Follow me," Ella said.

They pushed through, one at a time. On the other side of the curtain, the tunnel widened to twice its size. A few yards ahead, the cave came to an end, and sunlight poured in.

"The sun?" Ella furrowed her brow. "We're in a cave. How can it . . . ?" Her voice trailed off.

"How can it be sunny?" Richie finished her question. "It's the middle of the night!"

They stood up and dusted off their pants.

"Are we . . . Inside?"

"I think so," Richie said.

They stood in awe. Prairie dogs still raced around them. Richie straightened his giant eyeglasses and headed for the exit.

"C'mon," he said in a deep voice. "Let's find our friends."

Ella hurried to catch him. Together they stepped outside—outside into the Inside.

CHAPTER 29

INSIDE ARCTIC TOWN

Water rushed against Noah's face and pulled back his hair. His feet repeatedly slapped the walls and ceiling of the tunnel. Each time Podgy rounded a bend, Noah worried that he'd slip off the penguin's back and drown. He couldn't figure out where he was. Inside the block of ice? In the ground? Who had built this secret tunnel? And why?

Something brushed against his face. It was soft and smooth, like velvet. Just as Noah realized that he was about to run out of breath again, a spot of light appeared in the distance. Podgy worked his flippers harder than ever to gain speed. As they swam forward, the light grew continuously until Noah realized it was an opening in the ceiling of the cave. A beam of light streamed through the hole.

Podgy porpoised through the opening in a glistening arc of rainbow colors as water sprinkled around him in the sunlight. He landed belly first on a sheet of ice and skidded forward at full speed. Screaming, Noah rode atop Podgy as if he were on a toboggan that had veered out of control. Fifty feet ahead, they slid to a stop.

Noah lay still for several seconds, too stunned to speak. He wiped the icy water off his brow and looked around. Wherever he was, the place looked like the North Pole. They'd stopped in the middle of a frozen lake surrounded by snow-peaked mountains. Penguins were scattered everywhere. Noah saw them on the mountainsides—black freckles dotting the white hillside. The sky was blue and cloudless.

"Where am I?" Noah gasped.

Podgy couldn't answer, of course, but that was okay, because Noah figured it out himself. He was in Arctic Town—the real Arctic Town.

Podgy flapped his flippers briefly and waddled off in a rush. He looked like a normal penguin, not one that could shuttle a boy to a snowy fairyland. Rubbing his arms, Noah scurried up beside him.

"You *are* on my side." Noah surveyed the incredible snowy landscape and added, "Podgy, I'm freezing."

Another penguin, almost as large as Podgy, dashed between the two of them and dived into the ice hole that they'd just sailed out of.

"Where's he going?" Noah asked. "Not the zoo! Why would he—? Wait a minute! That's your replacement? He's taking your place . . . at the zoo . . . so nobody will notice that a penguin is missing!"

Podgy kept waddling forward.

"This explains the part in Megan's journal about seeing three bears instead of two. The third bear was Blizzard's replacement. They didn't change places fast enough, so they both were in the zoo at the same time!"

Podgy waved his flippers as if to indicate that Noah was on to something.

"Holy smokes! What is this place?"

Suddenly little tremors shook the ice. In the distance, something was charging toward them. Noah couldn't make out what it was.

"Uh . . . Podgy?" he mumbled. "Is that something we should be worried about?"

As the figure drew near, the ice downright quaked. When it finally shot into view, Noah discovered what it was. A polar bear.

"Blizzard!" Noah hollered with delight. He turned to Podgy and explained, "Blizzard and I—we've met."

Blizzard threw his snout toward the sky and roared. He

slowed down, but his footfalls continued to shake the ice and rock Podgy about. The king-size polar bear stopped in front of Noah and let out a friendly grunt. Noah reached out and stroked his fur as if he were a harmless pet. Blizzard nudged his snout against the boy's arm.

"I made it, Blizzard!"

Blizzard slowly lowered his stomach to the ground. His intention was clear: he wanted Noah to climb on his back. When Noah didn't move, the bear swung his big snout around and nudged the boy's rear end, bringing him closer.

"First Podgy, and now you?" Noah said. He grabbed two handfuls of fur, climbed up Blizzard's side, and mounted him like a horse. "Giddyup!"

Blizzard swiftly rose to his feet and pitched his weight forward. Noah felt the bear's massive muscles working beneath him.

"Heigh-ho! Blizzard away!"

Though Noah had said this as a joke, the bear broke into a serious run. With each lunge forward, Noah bounced up and down and sideways. Podgy scurried after them, trying to run but succeeding only in waddling quickly. With his flippers stretched out to his sides, he looked like a miniature airplane tooling down the runway.

Noah cupped his hands around his mouth and shouted, "C'mon, Podgy!"

The penguin raced after them, but he couldn't keep up.

"Blizzard," Noah said, "I need to get out of this cold!"

Blizzard growled and picked up speed. Noah glanced over his shoulder. Poor Podgy had shrunk into a black dot on the ice. Noah felt sorry for him—sorry that he'd been born a fat bird who couldn't fly.

Blizzard raced forward. A snowy shoreline appeared ahead, populated by a crowd of at least fifty penguins. When Blizzard approached, the birds were standing idle. Seconds later, Noah witnessed something remarkable. The penguins divided themselves into two equal groups, creating a narrow aisle between them. Then one small penguin waddled to the end of the aisle. He looked toward the sky, and the other penguins looked toward him. Suddenly he charged down the path. When he neared the edge of the crowd, the other penguins chased after him. Together the penguins raced across the ice.

"What's that?" Noah muttered. "A game?"

The small penguin jumped and flapped his flippers. Noah's eyes widened. His jaw dropped. The penguin started to fly! Not very high—perhaps five feet above the ice—but he was unmistakably airborne.

"No way!" Noah called from his bear-top view.

The bird struggled to stay in the air. As he beat his flippers, his body jerked . . . rose . . . dipped; jerked . . . rose . . . and dipped. He was sloppy and uncoordinated, but he managed to stay up. The other penguins leaped into the air, only to crash down to the ice, somersault, and tumble over one another.

"It's a flight school!" Noah said. "The penguins are learning to fly!"

Within seconds, all the penguins had crashed and turned into a mound of rolling blubber and flailing flippers. Only the small penguin managed to stay in the air for a while. He sailed as high as ten feet before he, too, crashed to the ice.

"No way!"

Blizzard slowed down at the shore of the frozen lake and stomped onto the frosty white land. He and Noah were surrounded on all sides by snow-covered hills and distant ice-capped mountains.

"Where are we going, Bliz? I need to—"

Noah's eyes focused on the details of the bright white landscape, and he found his answer. To the right, a huge igloo that had blended in with the snow became visible. At one end it had an arched opening, which Noah figured must be the doorway. Blizzard padded to the igloo, and Noah hunched down so they both could fit through the archway.

The igloo was warm. A colorful Oriental rug lay on the floor. A bundle of warm, dry clothing and a pile of blankets were heaped in the middle. Noah kicked up his legs and slid down Blizzard's side. Shivering, he walked to the bundle and found a note pinned to the blanket on top.

> *Noah,*
>
> *If you're reading this, then you got here early because I was hoping to meet you. This is the Igloo of Old. And if you're reading this, you're soaking wet! I asked the animals to round up a change of clothes for you. I'll see you in the City of Species. Podgy will show you the way. Remember to be careful! Don't let anyone stop you. You've come too far to turn back now.*
> *Good luck, little man!*
> *Tank*

"The City of Species?" Noah said. "What's that?"

He disregarded the note for the time being and reached for what was urgent: the bundle of warm, dry clothes. He picked up a fresh towel, big enough to cover a lion, and stripped off his wet jacket and shirt, shivering madly. When he undid the button on his pants, he looked at Blizzard and said, "Do you mind? I know you're a bear and everything, but still . . ."

Blizzard rolled his head to one side and gazed out the arched doorway.

"Thanks," Noah said.

He worked the towel over his body, rubbing vehemently. Once he was dry, he pulled two heavy blankets from the pile, dropped down on the rug, and dived between the folds of the covers.

"I'm so *c-c-cooo-ld-d*," he moaned.

Under the weight of the blankets, Noah was soon warmed by the heat of his own body.

Blizzard came near. At eye level, Noah had a clear view of his paws. They were big enough to stomp out a campfire, and his claws were sharp enough to slice a watermelon. The bear dropped his body and nudged in beside Noah.

Not a moment later, Podgy waddled through the entrance to the igloo.

"Hey, *P-P-Podgy*," Noah mumbled. "*N-n-nice* that you *c-c-could* make it."

Podgy aimed straight for the bundle. He snatched a blanket with his bill, turned around, walked on top of Noah, and dropped the cover evenly across his shoulders.

"*Th-th-thanks*, Podge!"

Noah nestled so close to Blizzard that his knees slipped into the bear's furry blubber. The great animal gently laid his head across Noah's body and wrapped him in his long neck. Noah could hear Blizzard breathing; he could even feel the bursts of warm air across his back. The chill continued to ease out of his body.

Noah realized how exhausted he was. It was the middle of the night at home—wherever that was. A quick nap would help him in his next adventure. He closed his eyes and dozed off, letting himself slip into dreamland.

In his mind, he found a memory of his sister and held it. He pictured Megan's face and her smile. Love for her filled his heart as he fell asleep in the warmth of his strange and wonderful new friends.

RICHIE DRAWS A CROWD

Ella and Richie stepped out of the cave and into a blast of hot air and blinding light. The landscape was dry and dusty. Cacti grew across the dry terrain, some with round stems that resembled prickly mittens and others with long stems like the pipes of a green organ. The ground was pitted with countless holes. Prairie dogs raced from one hole to another, kicking up clouds of dust as they dived recklessly in and out. The furry critters dashed around in erratic zigzags. They sprinted and stopped, sprinted and stopped, looking confused or surprised by every spot that their own paws carried them to.

Far across the plain, a strange light blinked on and off. Each surge displayed a new color—red, green, yellow, blue, and orange.

"What's that light?" Ella asked.

"I have no idea." Richie looked around and said, "Where are we?"

Ella scooped up a handful of dirt and let it sift through her fingers. "I don't know," she said, "but this place is dry and hot—and filled with gophers."

"Stop calling them gophers. They're prairie dogs."

"Whatever!" she said. "Look, Richie, I only know what you know. We crawled through some kind of secret tunnel and wound up here. This doesn't make sense to me either."

"Will any of this *ever* make sense?"

Ella thought about it. "I hope so. Maybe it will just take awhile. C'mon! Let's see what there is to see."

She started out across the flat terrain.

"Like the bear," Richie said, hurrying after her.

"The who?"

"The bear—the bear that went over the mountain. You know that song." He threw back his head and sang, "'The bear went over the mountain, the bear went over the mountain, the bear—'"

"Richie!"

"'—went over the mooouuunnn-TONNN . . . to see—'"

"Richie!"

"Okay, okay. Hold on a second." Richie reached into his backpack and pulled out his flashy metallic running shoes. They glittered in the sunlight. "Let me put on my walking feet first."

"Great," Ella moaned. "You're gonna blind the gophers."

Richie tied his shoelaces, and the scouts headed off. After a while, they stripped off their jackets and crammed them into Richie's backpack. In no time, sweat dripped from their brows, and their hair clung to their foreheads. Occasionally a prairie dog sat on its rear end and peered up at them. The hard, fixed stares of the rodents suggested that they expected something from the children. At one point, a gang of prairie dogs started to trail Richie. Their eyes were riveted on his running shoes. They chased his feet in little zigzags, stopping and starting abruptly and crashing into one another.

"Look, Richie! You have a fan club!" Ella exclaimed.

"Yeah. What's up with that?"

"I guess you're not the only one who likes those shoes."

Richie glanced at his heels. "You think they like my shoes?"

"Well," Ella said with a smile, "they shine more than your personality does. That's for sure."

Richie took a few steps forward and watched the animals rush around his shoes again. As the scouts made their way across the dry landscape, more and more prairie dogs tagged along behind him. Glancing over his shoulder and under his arm, Richie kept an inventory of the animals. They seemed mesmerized by and afraid of his shoes at the same time.

The group advanced steadily. In the dry terrain, they passed cacti shaped like pitchforks, walked through thin patches of knee-high grass, and maneuvered around countless holes made by prairie dogs. As Richie walked, his slick shoes sparkled in the sunlight. More than a hundred prairie dogs were now chasing him, running in spurts that loosely matched the movement of his feet. Every so often, a prairie dog darted between Ella's legs or across her toes, prompting her to holler, "Hey!" or "Bad gopher!"

The scouts continued their journey across the barren plain, passing strange, oddly shaped cacti and kicking up clouds of dust. Eventually they reached the light. For a light with such a bright and powerful beam, it was unexpectedly small—about the size of an orange. Ella looked at Richie. Every time the light blinked, he was saturated in a new color.

When the blue color flashed, she said, "You look like a Smurf."

Richie shot her a scornful look and stuck out his tongue, which turned green in the simultaneous flash of green light.

Below the light was a curtain—purple and velvet, with yellow tassels hanging beneath it. It looked like the curtain they'd seen at the Chamber of Lights.

"Look familiar?" Ella asked.

"Yep."

The curtain was fastened to a rod, but the rod, like the light, wasn't fastened to anything. It just hovered in the air.

"Who does the decorating around this place?" Ella said. "Houdini?"

Beside the curtain was an old wooden sign that stood on a single post. It read, END OF SECTOR 62. "Sector Sixty-two?" Richie asked.

"No clue," Ella said.

"Should we go through the curtain," Richie asked, "or around it?"

"You decide."

Richie shrugged his shoulders and decided to walk beside it. Suddenly his head snapped back as if he'd walked into a wall. He staggered and dropped on his rear end.

"Whoa!" Ella said. "You okay? What happened?"

She reached out and touched the space beside the curtain. The space touched her back! It *was* a wall—a wall painted to look exactly like the desert they were in. It felt soft and gooey, like Jell-O. Ella pushed her palm forward, and the wall gooped over her fingertips. Then it firmed up and spit out her hand.

"What in the world?"

The paint was gone from the spot that she'd touched, and a black handprint had replaced it. Then, like magic, fresh paint appeared and the handprint melted away. The image on the strange wall had restored itself. Ella looked down at her hand. Sure enough, some sort of paint was smeared all over it.

"Eeew!" She wiped the gunk off on her pants. "Gross!"

Richie was covered with paint splotches. His face was as blue as the sky, and his legs looked as yellowy brown as the desert plain. He stood up and wiped the gunk off his nose, saying, "So much for going around it."

"I guess that means we go through it," Ella said.

Richie wiped his hands on the back of his pants. "Ladies first," he said.

She shook the tension out of her shoulders, gingerly stepped forward, and grumbled, "Always the gentleman," as she pulled back the curtain.

❧ CHAPTER 31 ❧
ACROSS SECTOR 24

Noah woke and casually stretched. He opened his eyes, expecting to find the usual contents of his room, but instead discovering a one-ton polar bear lying beside him. He sprang to his feet.

"What—? Where am I?"

He first thought that his room had turned magically into an igloo overnight. Then he remembered where he was and all the crazy events that had brought him here.

Blizzard was also waking from a nap. The bear rolled over, reached out his massive paws, and yawned. Nearby, Podgy stood like an attentive soldier. Noah looked down and realized he was naked. He crossed his legs and dropped his hands in front of himself.

"Guys!" he said. "You mind?"

Blizzard and Podgy turned their heads. Noah scooped up his clothes and discovered that they were soaking wet.

"Oh great."

He picked up his watch and saw the water had ruined it. The once-glowing digits were now dim.

"More good news."

He went to the pile of dry clothing and rummaged through it.

"Where did you guys find this stuff?" he asked.

He pulled out jeans, a sweatshirt, a jacket, insulated underwear, purple snow pants, yellow boots, a red hunting cap with earflaps as big and round as pancakes, and a green poncho. When he was dressed, he held his arms out to his sides and faced his new friends.

"How do I look?"

Blizzard buried his snout in his paws. Podgy looked away and tilted his bill in the air. Noah rolled his eyes in disgust.

He walked to the door and looked outside. How long had he slept? He didn't know, but judging by how groggy he felt, he guessed it wasn't much more than a half hour. Back home, it probably was around one o'clock in the morning.

"We'd better go," he said. "I'm not sure how much time we've lost."

The band of three slipped out into the cold. Blizzard hunched down, inviting Noah to climb onto his back. Noah looked at the large penguin beside him.

"Is there room for Podgy? Podgy, can you climb up there?"

Podgy looked from Blizzard to the ground, considering Noah's question. Then he waddled forward and, with as much energy as he could muster, leaped up, managing only to smack his belly against Blizzard's furry side.

"Try again, Podge," Noah said. "This time I'll help you."

When Podgy jumped again, Noah grabbed his blubbery rear end and pushed him up.

"Holy smokes, Podge! How much you weigh?" he moaned.

Flapping his flippers and rolling his body like a caterpillar, Podgy squirmed and heaved his way onto Blizzard's back. He settled precariously right behind the bear's head.

Noah scaled Blizzard's side and sat behind Podgy. He wrapped his arms around the penguin's middle and grabbed the bear's neck. Podgy closed his flippers around Noah's forearms. The two of them looked as though they were cuddling together.

"Yeah," Noah said. "This will work." He tapped Blizzard's neck. "C'mon, big guy! Let's ride out of here!"

Blizzard growled and headed off, his big paws flattening the snow. Less than five minutes later, a storm rose up. Snow started to fall sideways, and the wind beat against them. Within a matter of minutes, the igloo had disappeared behind them in a sea of white. Noah was thankful for his winter hat, regardless of how ridiculous it looked.

After walking for a half hour, Blizzard reached a hill and began to climb. As they advanced, Noah saw penguins huddled in icy hillside crevices, sheltering themselves from the storm. The three of them reached the crest and, from there, saw a light blinking in the snowy valley below.

Using an outward-facing palm, Noah shielded his face from the cold push of the snow and wind. "Is that where we're headed?" He had to raise his voice above the noisy storm.

Blizzard growled and swung his head in a circle. He immediately started the decline, bouncing Podgy around like a plump infant on a jittery knee. The hill was so steep that Noah was afraid Blizzard would slip and send them snowballing into the valley below. Penguins scattered when they found themselves in Blizzard's path. And for the first time, Noah saw another kind of animal: arctic foxes. Their coats were as white and clean as the blowing snow. They raced about in all directions, leaping over snowy drifts and ducking into dark crevices.

At the bottom of the hill, the light was so bright that Noah had to shield his eyes. It flashed a new color across the white landscape every few seconds. Directly beneath it hung an orange curtain with wild green tassels. The curtain was suspended from a rod, which, in turn, was held up by nothing at all. The curtain rod dangled in the air like a magic trick.

"That's impossible," Noah said.

But at this point, he knew that nothing was impossible. They passed a snow-covered sign, and Blizzard paused. Noah reached down and brushed off the snow. The wooden sign was carved with large black letters: END OF SECTOR 24.

"Sector Twenty-four?"

Blizzard jerked his nose up to the sky and let out a deafening roar. Covering his head with his arms, Noah worried that the snowy mountains might avalanche. A moment later, the bear drove the velvet curtain back with his snout and stepped into it. The curtain slid across Noah's back and closed off the storm behind them.

CHAPTER 32

CITY OF SPECIES
POPULATION: GROWING

Ella and Richie stood in awe, with several prairie
dogs at their feet. They'd entered a city that seemed to
have been built by the most potent pieces of a hundred
imaginations. It was situated in the middle of a dense forest. Buildings and trees shared the streets in equal numbers, just feet or inches apart from one another. In some
places, trees grew inside buildings, and their branches
jutted through walls and windows, making the buildings
appear to be giant metal tree forts. Everywhere the scouts
looked, the city and the forest seemed to need each other,
as if one couldn't exist without the other.

Each building was a different size, shape, and design. Some were steel and iron, some marble and stone, and others nothing but glass. Brick sidewalks ran in all directions, leading to doorsteps, disappearing into mysterious alleys, or traversing patches of flowery bushes. Treetops functioned as rooftops, bamboo chutes worked as downspouts, and branches served as signposts. The place before them was a strange and stunning union of forest and city.

Water flowed throughout the city. Streams ran in the middle of sidewalks. Waterfalls cascaded down tall glass buildings and splashed into fountains below. Clouds of mist drifted through the streets.

Besides all this, the city contained something even more spectacular: animals—thousands of them. They crowded everywhere and rushed in all directions. Zebras, tigers, camels, pandas, hippos—every animal imaginable. Ella glimpsed a family of giraffes striding down a street, bobbing their heads to miss electrical wires. Then a crowd of bears caught her eye; they had stopped at an intersection to let three slow-moving tortoises pass. She looked up and saw hundreds of flying squirrels leaping through trees and across rooftops.

The city had its share of people, too. They seemed to be going about normal, everyday business. Groups stood at storefronts, reading posters. Individuals sat on balconies, talking in groups and drinking from colorful mugs. Some meandered along the sidewalks, carrying flowers and bags and books and babies. Others rode animals. One woman was carried by a lion, a man rode an ostrich, and an entire family sat atop an elephant. As the riders passed her, they looked as casual and ho-hum as they would be if they were in ordinary cars.

"Richie," Ella said, "what's going on?"

High above them was a complicated web of glass tunnels. Some narrow and others wide, they wove through the buildings and trees. They all were filled with fresh, churning water and a mixture of sea creatures—fish, crabs, and turtles. The tunnels carried these water animals across the streets, from one place to another. Ella watched a bizarre rainbow of fish jump through an opening in a tunnel roof and splash down in a nearby fountain.

Velvet curtains hung in front of doorways. They looked like the curtain that the scouts had just pushed through, but each one was a different color. Near every curtain was a sign. Ella could read some of them from where she stood. They announced different sectors, whatever those were: SECTOR 38, SECTOR 32, SECTOR 28, SECTOR 5, SECTOR 47. She watched a gang of alligators push through the curtain beside a SECTOR 14 sign and join the dreamy herds of animals on the street.

Richie mumbled, stuttered, and made noises like

"What—? Wh-wh-what—? Er . . . what?" He sounded like a worn-out moped.

Four elephants stomped by. They shook the ground with a force so great that the children bounced. This made Richie's shoes sparkle in the sunlight and catch the attention of two anteaters, who raced up and sniffed his toes, jabbing at his feet with their long, tubular snouts.

"Hey!" Richie said.

He jumped to avoid them. Their tongues flicked in and out, snapping at his heels. When they realized that Richie's shoes weren't edible, they gave up and walked off, working their snouts like vacuums to suck bugs off the street.

A moment later, more members of Richie's prairie dog fan club scampered through the curtain and surrounded him. They sat up on their small rumps and dangled their front legs in front of their pudgy bellies.

Ella looked down and said, "Don't you gophers have any holes to dig?"

A couple of prairie dogs yipped defiantly. Ella turned her attention back to the city. Above the treetops, the sky was blue—so spotlessly blue that it looked fake. She even suspected that it might be. Perhaps it wasn't even the sky—at least not the one she'd always known.

The air was filled with birds. Some, small and colorful, feverishly worked their wings. Others, large and gray, coasted on their wide wingspans. They dived down to the street and flew back into the sky, moving in elegant sweeps that seemed choreographed. Monkeys landed on ledges, jumped back into the forest, sat on balconies and awnings, and hitched rides on the backs of elephants and rhinos.

Ella read a wooden sign that dangled from a tree:

CITY OF SPECIES

POPULATION: GROWING

"I think this is it," Ella said. "I think we made it."

"Yeah." Richie pushed his glasses up on his nose. "But made it where?"

Ella shrugged her shoulders. "All I know is, Megan's here. Noah, too. If we—" She thrust her arm forward and pointed across the street. "Hey! That guy look like anyone we know?"

A lanky man was strolling along the sidewalk. He had red hair and a splash of ugly freckles.

"That's Charlie Red!" said Richie. "The guy from Creepy Critters!"

"Hide!" Ella said.

The two of them swung around a tree trunk and peered out.

"Ugh," Ella moaned. "I knew we'd see more of that jerk."

Charlie Red checked his watch and seemed to become angry with himself, as if he'd suddenly remembered something important. He leaped over a line of rabbits and wove through a group of peacocks—a variety of obstacles on a motley challenge course. He disappeared behind a pink curtain dangling under a wooden sign marked SECTOR 17.

As the two of them stepped away from the tree, a gorilla swung off an overhead branch and landed in front of Richie and Ella with a ground-shaking thud. Massive and muscular, he was covered in shiny black fur. As he eyed the children, he cocked his head back and forth, raised his huge, hairy arms, and grunted five times in quick succession. Then, emitting a long, low rumble, he pounded his fists against his chest. When he finally dropped his arms and stopped his noise, he headed straight for Richie, swinging his immense shoulders and dragging his knuckles on the street.

"Um . . . Ella?" said Richie.

"Don't sweat it. He's not gonna hurt you."

"Easy for you to say—I'm the one he's staring at."

When the gorilla reached Richie, he leaned in so closely that his breath blew back the hair on the boy's forehead. Ella caught a whiff of the beast's breath from where she stood. It smelled like rotten bananas.

"Hey, Richie," Ella said. "We finally found someone with breath worse than yours."

The gorilla snorted and wriggled his flat nose. He opened his mouth, proudly revealing his collection of yellow teeth.

Richie took a step back, causing his running shoes to reflect the sunlight. The gorilla saw the sparkle, squatted, and stared at the glittery footwear. He poked the heel with his thick finger and flinched. He looked apprehensively from Richie's face to his shoes. Suddenly he lurched forward, seized the boy by the waist, and threw him over his shoulder. Grunting loudly, he stripped off the shoes. Then he dropped the shoeless boy on the ground, whirled around, and bolted off. The scouts caught their last glimpse of him tearing through a crowd of ostriches, waving the glittery sneakers in the air.

Richie sat up and looked around with a stunned expression on his pale face.

"What happened?" he mumbled. He stuck out his feet and wiggled his toes. "My shoes!"

Ella giggled. "I've heard of a purse snatcher, but never a sneaker snatcher."

The prairie dogs gathered around Richie and balanced on their rear ends with their small paws dangling in front of them. They glanced from his face to his feet, confused and slightly forlorn.

"Sorry, guys," Richie said as he rummaged through his backpack for his boots. "I've been robbed."

Most of the prairie dogs turned and marched back toward Sector 62, disappointed. The ones that stayed—about a dozen—scurried forward and sniffed Richie's feet.

"Careful, gophers!" Ella warned the prairie dogs. She pinched her nose to elaborate.

"I can't believe it—robbed by a gorilla," Richie whimpered as he laced his boots. "It doesn't make any—"

A voice rang out. "That's them!"

Standing in front of the Sector 17 curtain and pointing a trembling finger at the scouts was Charlie Red. He raised a walkie-talkie to his big lips and shouted, "I've got a code red at Seventeen Sector! Repeat! I've got a security breach in the city at Seventeen Sector! All available police-monkeys, please report!"

In response to his words, dozens of monkeys darted out of a dark alley behind Sector 17. Some charged across the street, while others raced from tree branch to tree branch. Unlike the monkeys the scouts had seen earlier, these looked menacing—even deadly. They had their mouths open wide and their fangs drawn back like blades. Their stares were piercing. They were howling, screeching, or chanting, *"Oou! Oou! Oou!"*

"Richie! RUN!" Ella shouted.

Richie jumped to his feet, and the scouts dashed down the street.

Charlie Red continued to call for help into his walkie-talkie. "I repeat! We have a security breach near One-Seven Sector. All available units, report now!"

As the scouts ran, Ella noticed something peculiar. Off to the side a polar bear was walking in the same direction. On his back were a penguin and a strange-looking kid dressed in purple snow pants and a red cap. For a second, she thought the boy looked familiar.

~❧ CHAPTER 33 ☙~

A Bear, a Penguin,
and a Squad of Police-Monkeys

As Blizzard lumbered through the City of Species, Noah studied the sights around him. It was as if he'd stepped into a fairy tale about the union of humans and animals, city and nature. He tilted his head upward and watched hundreds of birds fly above the city. They soared through the open spots in the sky, wove through buildings, and flipped across branches in deeply meshed tree limbs. Their shadows crossed the streets, more like dark wedges of matter than spots emptied of light. Noah felt as if he could reach out and scoop their shadows up.

Blizzard strolled past tigers, wolverines, and a family of

rhinos. An elephant used its trunk to pick leaves off tree branches. A kangaroo hopped onto a tortoise's shell to sniff a fat possum dangling upside down from a branch.

Noah noticed velvet curtains like the one he'd just stepped through hanging in front of doorways. Beside each curtain, a wooden sign announced a different sector.

"These sectors," Noah muttered. "They connect the City Zoo to this place. But how?"

A gorilla bumped into Blizzard. The bear growled, but the gorilla ignored him and kept rushing by. Noah noticed something peculiar—the gorilla was carrying a pair of strangely familiar running shoes.

Seconds later, Noah heard a man's voice shouting something about a "security breach." He glanced over his shoulder. There was Charlie Red! The nasty security guard from Creepy Critters was yelling orders into a walkie-talkie. Simultaneously a squad of monkeys charged out of a dark alley into the street.

Beside Blizzard, a father scooped up his young daughter and said to his wife, "Something's wrong! Police-monkeys are on alert!"

Noah looked at Podgy with a furrowed brow. "Police-monkeys?"

The monkeys charged through the city, weaving through the other animals. One jumped over the back of a lion. Another darted between the tall legs of a giraffe.

A third hurdled a koala and a mailbox in a single bound. Some were langurs like Mr. Tall Tail, with thick, cartoonish eyebrows and patchy, unkempt beards growing from their cheeks. Others were stern-faced baboons. Even Charlie Red looked apish, the way he was jumping around. Noah almost expected him to jump onto a tree branch and start scratching his armpits.

"Who are they chasing? I don't see—"

But then Noah *did* see. Ella and Richie were running down the sidewalk. Charlie Red's squad of police-monkeys was chasing *them*!

"No!" Noah gasped. He slapped Blizzard on the side and said, "Blizzard! My friends are here. They're in trouble!"

Blizzard didn't waste a moment. He charged across the street. Every animal smaller than a truck ducked out of his way. It was obvious to all that Blizzard meant business.

"Go, Blizzard!" Noah yelled.

As the polar bear charged, Podgy bounced around like a pillow on a bull. At one point, he shot into the air, and Noah had to snag his flipper and pull him back. Watching the chase, Noah noticed a curious thing. Monkeys weren't the only animals chasing his friends. So were prairie dogs! He dismissed his confusion for the time being and called out, "Ella! Richie!"

They didn't hear him. The two scouts darted through one of the velvet curtains. An overhead sign read, SECTOR 13. Blizzard pursued them, nearly trampling a few prairie dogs. Beside the curtain, Noah read a sign that said, NO ADMITTANCE FOR THE UNWINGED!

"The unwinged?" Noah asked. "What's that?"

But roaring his thunderous roar, Blizzard was already pounding through the velvet drape.

❧ CHAPTER 34 ☙

THE UNEXPECTED CLIFF

As the curtain closed behind the scouts, Richie asked, "What's Sector Thirteen?"

"I don't know and I don't care!" Ella answered. "Just keep me away from those monkeys!"

Accompanied by prairie dogs, they found themselves scrambling down a short, gloomy hallway. The hallway ended on a wooden platform that jutted into a bright space. As the scouts raced onto the platform, Ella skidded to a stop just inches from the platform's edge, beyond which the Earth disappeared. Far below, Ella saw a deep fog. Her heart stammered as she realized that she'd just missed falling over a cliff—a cliff in the middle of what she'd thought was flat land.

"Richie!" She flung her arm out to the side and slammed Richie across the chest. Richie's feet flew forward, and he crashed down on his back. Ella leaned out and again gazed over the cliff. The faraway fog looked menacing.

"No way," she muttered. "There's just no way."

As Blizzard charged down the hallway, Noah tried to figure out the meaning of the sign he'd just read: NO ADMITTANCE FOR THE UNWINGED!

"The unwinged," Noah said. "The unwinged, the unwinged, the unwinged . . . I don't get it."

Podgy's beady black eyes stared intently into Noah's. He pointed his flippers out to his sides and flapped them deliberately. Noah raised his eyebrows.

"Oh no," he murmured. "It's the Forest of Flight, the *real* one."

Ella had little more than a second to look around and realize what they'd nose-dived into. Sector 13 was some type of birdhouse—a birdhouse the size of a stadium. But this birdhouse seemed to be bottomless. Below her feet, the cliff fell and fell, ending in a distant fog that concealed its true depth. From the ocean of fog rose hundreds of trees. They were too long and thick to be anything but magical. The birdhouse was circular, and its walls were dressed in green ivy. Overhead Ella saw a glass dome, and beyond that, the strange blue sky she'd seen in the City of Species. All around her, waterfalls spilled over mossy cliffs and burst into mist as they splashed across boulders. Thousands of birds soared through the air and skipped across tree branches—birds of so many sizes and colors that Ella thought they looked like bits of a rainbow.

Ella's attention abruptly returned to her predicament when a prairie dog came racing from behind her. It skidded, trying to stop before the cliff, but was unsuccessful and fell over the edge with a fearful screech. A moment later, another prairie dog followed suit. Then a third, and a fourth. One after the other, they all skidded and disappeared. Ella had no time to stop them. It took only seconds for every prairie dog that had followed Richie to fall over the edge. She could do nothing but scream.

From his high perch on Blizzard's back, Noah spotted his friends at the edge of a cliff. For some reason, Richie was lying on his back. Then a terrible thing happened: one by one, the prairie dogs that had been chasing them tumbled over the edge.

Blizzard hotfooted along, reaching the scouts so suddenly that his huge paw barely missed planting Richie's head in the ground like an oversized seed. Noah jumped down and rushed to Ella, who was on her hands and knees, looking over the cliff.

"Ella!" he called. He gazed over the edge. The prairie dogs looked like falling dots as they headed down to the fog.

"I couldn't stop them!" she explained. "I couldn't!"

Noah knew he had to do something—but what? He sprang to his feet and scanned the ivy-covered walls of the building. In his search for a solution, he noticed something directly in front of him, across the great distance of the Forest of Flight. A single hole was carved in the wall beneath a small blinking light. On the basis of everything Noah had experienced, he was certain that the hole led to the Clarksville City Zoo.

"It's a tunnel," he said. "A tunnel that gets birds from *that* zoo to *this* zoo—like the one Podgy and I came through. The day I met Marlo at the Clarksville Zoo . . . all those birds . . . they came from here." But he had no time to think about that now. He looked toward the treetops, whistled, and called, "Marlo! Are you here? *Marlo!*"

A tiny blue bird shot out from the leaves as quickly as a pellet from a gun. He landed on Noah's shoulder and stared at him.

"Marlo!"

Still distraught from the sight of the falling prairie dogs, Ella jumped up. "This is *that* bird? The one that came to your window?"

"This is Marlo in the flesh—er . . . feathers, I guess." Noah pointed to the prairie dogs and said, "Marlo, we need help!"

With a few lightning-quick jerks of his head, Marlo assessed the situation. He chirped twice and launched back up to the treetops.

"What's he doing?" Ella asked. "He's going the wrong way!"

"I don't know. But we need to trust him. He's smart."

"Smart is good, but we need fast." Ella looked down. The prairie dogs had disappeared into the fog.

Marlo dived out of the sky and zipped past in a blue blur. Seconds later, thousands of birds burst from the treetops. They raced after Marlo, creating a gust of wind so powerful that branches and leaves ripped into the air. The wind blew back Ella's ponytail and flapped the earflaps on Noah's cap. Richie clung to Blizzard's leg.

Noah stood and watched; after all, he'd seen this before. Birds of every family and species descended: eagles, owls, vultures, falcons, hawks, and chickadees. Swarms of hummingbirds, as colorful as crayons and not much bigger, dived into the depths of the birdhouse.

Noah cried, "Get 'em, guys!"

Together the three scouts peered into the wondrous tree-filled abyss and watched the endless stream of birds race after the falling prairie dogs.

"I can't believe this!" Richie exclaimed. "They say the

early bird catches the worm. What kind of bird catches a prairie dog?"

Noah was about to answer when he heard a droning sound. Ella and Richie heard it, too. Even Blizzard perked up his ears, and Podgy cocked his head. The sound was distant, but there was no mistaking what it was: paws beating the ground.

"Monkeys," Richie whispered.

Noah walked to the middle of the platform. To the left was a gate that led to a narrow bamboo ramp. The ramp skimmed the interior wall of the birdhouse, winding around until it disappeared into the trees. It looked like a special access ramp—a quick way to get from the platform to other sections of the Forest of Flight. Whatever the ramp was intended for, it was too narrow and unsteady to be for general use.

"Where does that thing go?" Noah asked.

"It doesn't matter," Richie said. "We're too heavy. It'll collapse if we try to walk on it."

"What if we run superfast?" Noah said.

"Don't be stupid! This isn't a cartoon."

"It's either that or we wait here for the monkeys." Noah climbed on Blizzard's back, taking his seat behind Podgy. "It's our best shot."

Blizzard growled, seconding Noah's idea. Ella silently climbed up behind Noah.

"I don't like this," Richie said. "Not at all!"

But he clambered up Blizzard's furry side and plopped down in the last available seat—near the bear's rump. Blizzard charged through the gate and raced onto the bamboo ramp, carrying the scouts away from Charlie Red and his threatening squad of police-monkeys.

⚜ CHAPTER 35 ⚜

THE BATTLE IN THE TREETOPS

"Hurry, Blizzard!" Richie called out. "I see the police-monkeys!"

Blizzard dropped his head and raced forward. The bamboo stalks were strong, but Noah wondered how long the ramp could support them. He looked over his shoulder and watched the monkeys charge out of the dark hallway. Some of them stopped to watch the extraordinary spectacle of birds, but most chased after the scouts, quickly gaining ground on them.

"They're too fast!" Ella yelled.

A moment later, the birds that were flying alongside the

scouts swooped upward with a deafening cacophony of squawks and whistles, but nothing bothered Blizzard. He kept his head low and barreled forward, pounding down on his meaty paws and slicing his claws into the bamboo stalks.

Ella looked down. Five black falcons were rising from the depths of the birdhouse. They were flying more slowly than the other birds, and with good reason: each one had a prairie dog in its talons. Seven eagles trailed the falcons, following suit.

"They got 'em!" Ella shouted over the noise.

Most of the furry animals were bug-eyed and terrified, but some looked quite relaxed considering the monstrous drop they'd just endured. Together the eagles and falcons coasted up and above the bamboo ramp and safely dropped the prairie dogs near Blizzard.

"Yes!" Ella exclaimed.

"I thought you couldn't stand those prairie dogs," Richie said.

She shrugged her shoulders. "Danger makes me sensitive, I guess."

Blizzard didn't slow down for the prairie dogs. He dodged them as if they were ordinary obstacles in his path—not living things he could make go *splat*!

Noah looked around and pointed. "We're in trouble!"

Half of the band of monkeys was leaping through the

trees, lunging from branch to branch, while the others stayed behind.

"They're gonna head us off!" Ella announced. "We'll be cornered!"

The scouts could do nothing but charge forward. Noah watched as the monkeys caught up to them and passed them, still in the branches above. A few minutes later, the speedy animals dropped to the ramp a hundred feet ahead of the scouts. Seeing himself surrounded, Blizzard stopped and growled menacingly. He swung his head in long, slow arcs, assessing the situation and displaying his bone-crushing teeth.

"What are we gonna do?" Richie yelled. "What do these stupid monkeys want with us, anyway?"

Noah didn't know the answer, but he knew he didn't trust the monkeys. They were under Charlie Red's command, and Charlie Red was keeping Noah away from Megan. Charlie Red was one of the bad guys.

"We're trapped," Ella said.

Marlo flew down from the treetops and landed on Noah's shoulder, chirping hysterically.

"Marlo! What should we do?" Noah asked.

The kingfisher glanced at the police-monkeys and flew back into the trees. The monkeys closed to within seventy-five feet of the scouts, from behind and ahead.

"What now?" Ella asked.

"Charge through 'em, Bliz!" Noah commanded. "It's our best shot."

The polar bear raised his chin and growled. He threw back his weight, ready to charge forward. Suddenly— *Craack! Crrraackkk! Crrraaacckkk!* The bamboo beneath his rear paws snapped, and the broken strips dangled toward the fog below. The scouts screamed. The prairie dogs scattered in all directions.

"The ramp!" Ella shrieked. "It's falling apart!"

Noah's eyes darted to the treetops, and he willed Marlo to return. "C'mon, Marlo!" he moaned. "We need help somehow! We need help *now*!"

Crrraaacckkk! The bamboo snapped again beneath Blizzard's weight. The bear's front legs lurched through the planks and dangled precariously over the abyss. Pieces of bamboo plummeted, ricocheted off branches, and whirled away, out of control.

"Everyone off Blizzard!" Noah yelled.

The monkeys closed to within thirty feet on both sides. The crazy creatures didn't care that the ramp was breaking up.

"Move!" Noah shouted again. "Off! Off! Off!"

As the scouts rolled off Blizzard's back, the birds swooped out of the trees and swept down on the monkeys. They poked them with their bills and claws, trying to protect the scouts. Even Marlo plunged into the action. The tiny blue bird dived at a monkey and prodded its rear end with his pointy beak until it howled, leaped up, and fell right off the ramp. With their long, hairy arms waving wildly, the monkeys screeched and slapped at the birds.

A flock of woodpeckers gathered in a nearby tree. All at once, like pickaxes, their beaks began to hammer a branch in a blur of ultra swift motion. A cloud of wood splinters and sawdust filled the air.

Ella scrutinized them. "I don't like the looks of this," she said.

"What are they doing?" Richie asked.

"Heck if I know," Noah said. "But when that thing falls, it's gonna land on top of us."

The scouts scattered. All around them, the birds continued their chaotic attack on the monkeys, while the long-armed animals chanted, *"Oou! Oou! Oou!"* and slapped the air. *Crrraaaaccckkk!* Another bamboo stalk snapped in two. Struggling to stand up on the splintering planks, Blizzard groaned. Now he was frightened.

The woodpeckers hammered deeper into the branch. It trembled ominously.

"Get up, Blizzard!" Noah shouted.

Skrrackkk! Skrrrackkk! Skkkrrraaackkk! Cracking noises filled the air. The sound meant only one thing—the tree branch was splitting, and in a matter of moments, it would crash down on top of the great bear.

Finally Blizzard managed to lift his back paws and free them from the holes.

"Get up! Get up! Get up!" Noah shouted.

The branch twisted downward, and the woodpeckers scattered. Seconds later, *Ssskkkrrraaaccckkk!* The branch split in two.

"*Blizzard!*" the scouts yelled in one voice.

As the tree limb plummeted through the air, Blizzard freed his front paws and lunged forward. When the branch hit, a shock wave rocked the ramp. Everyone—the monkeys, the prairie dogs, Podgy, Blizzard, and the scouts—bounced and flailed out of control.

"Hold on!" Ella screamed.

The ramp rolled up and down, waving in the air for what seemed like an eternity. When it finally stopped moving, Noah scanned the scene to figure out what had happened. The fallen branch was wedged between the birdhouse wall and two other branches. It had become a secure bridge from the ramp to a distant tree. The woodpeckers had provided the scouts with an escape route!

For a minute, nobody moved except the birds that had been attacking the monkeys. Confused, they circled above the scene.

Then, as if someone had flicked a switch, the animals remembered what they had been doing and picked up where they'd left off. The birds dived down at the police-monkeys. The monkeys screeched in response and swatted the air.

The scouts ran to the fallen branch. Ella was the first to climb on, yelling, "C'mon, you guys! It's solid!"

Noah jumped on the bridge. "Blizzard, it's strong enough for you!"

He was contemplating how to get Podgy across when he noticed that Richie had already taken care of the logistics. He had placed his backpack between Blizzard's jaws and given its place on his back to Podgy. The penguin was riding piggyback! He'd wrapped his flippers over Richie's shoulders and wedged his feet in the crooks of his arms. His beak stuck out above Richie's forehead. Together they looked like an extraordinary creature with two mismatched faces. Podgy nervously snapped his head back and forth, slapping his bill against Richie's crown. His bill was like a pinball flipper and Richie's head the defenseless ball.

Ella and Noah quickly crossed the branch. The bridge was wide enough for Blizzard to plod over it without much difficulty. Even Richie and Podgy traversed it in a snap, though they were slightly wobblier than the others. As soon as everyone was safely planted on a sturdy, wide branch in the new tree, the woodpeckers descended on the fallen branch and started to work their red-plumed heads like miniature jackhammers.

"Now what are they doing?" Ella asked.

"Cutting through," Richie replied. "They're gonna get rid of the bridge so the monkeys can't get us—at least not without finding a different route."

"They're buying us time," Noah said.

Crrraackkk! The gigantic branch snapped in two. The scouts watched bark, twigs, and leaves plummet toward the distant fog, bouncing off other branches and sending tremors through the trees. Eventually all the pieces disappeared into the silence of the fog below.

Minutes passed. The scouts clung to their branch and waited. Noah had to determine their next move. They needed more help from the animals, but he worried that they might be on their own from now on.

Then, from the depths of the Forest of Flight, a roar rumbled. Before everyone's eyes, the fog shifted and shimmered. It was breaking up. One by one, an army of unusual birds pierced through the wall of fog and rose toward the scouts. The cloudy air swirled around their wings like smoke on a windy day.

"Now what are we dealing with?" Ella said.

"This is part of Marlo's plan," Noah replied.

Ella slumped against a small branch, confused and dull-eyed.

"Don't you get it? We've got a ride off this tree." He stuck out his thumb and called, "Taxi!"

❧ CHAPTER 36 ❧

The Return of the Dodo

hen the scouts had their first clear view of the new birds, Ella asked, "What are they? They look weird."

"Impossible!" Richie answered. "Those are dodo birds."

"*What* birds?" said Ella.

"Dodos."

Ella added her usual two-second sarcasm. "Dodo as in Richie?"

Noah said, "Dodo as in *extinct*. Right, Richie?"

"Yep," Richie said. "The dodo's been extinct for hundreds of years."

"With a name like dodo, I'm not surprised," Ella said.

"Dodos weren't stupid; they were just really nice," Richie explained. "A long time ago, sailors discovered them on an island. The sailors hunted the dodos, and they brought animals—rats, pigs, and dogs—that fed on their eggs. On top of this, the sailors wiped out the dodos' habitat to build homes. The birds' innocence made them easy victims, and they were killed in such numbers that it took less than a hundred years for the too-good-for-its-own-good dodo species to be wiped out."

"That's about the most disturbing thing I've ever heard," Ella said.

"I know," Richie said. "Poor birds."

"I'm not talking about the dodos, you dodo. I'm talking about the fact that you know that kind of stuff."

"Wait a minute," Noah cut in. "You guys are missing the most important part. The dodo is extinct."

"Yep," Richie said. He snatched his backpack from Blizzard's jaws and strapped it across his back.

"If they're extinct, how can we be watching a whole flock of them fly right up to us?"

"Good question," Richie said, "because not only is the dodo extinct, but it can't fly."

"Wait," Ella said. "This doesn't make any sense."

"The dodo is . . . well . . . truly a dodo about flying." Richie poked his thumb in Podgy's direction and added, "Like the penguin, it's a flightless bird."

"That solves it, then," Ella said. "Those things aren't dodos. You're wrong."

"Nunh-unh—I'm positive about this."

"Well, Mr. Britannica, do you mind telling me how an extinct bird that can't fly is flying around being . . . not extinct?"

Richie shrugged his shoulders.

The giant flock of dodos rose in front of them. They dipped and circled.

"They're definitely dodos!" Richie called out over the noise of their flapping wings.

Noah thought the birds resembled oversized seagulls. Their feathers were different shades of gray, and they had strange hooked beaks. Their unique feature was their ridiculously small wingspan.

A team of six dodos was carrying a velvet curtain like those the scouts had seen hanging at the entrances to the sectors. They draped it near Blizzard, across the branch. The bear looked at them as if to say, "Yeah? So what?"

"Step on the curtain, Blizzard," Noah said. "I think I know what they're doing."

Blizzard growled in protest. Then, realizing the dodos' intention, he complied. The big birds buried their claws in the cloth and, flapping their puny wings as fast as possible, hoisted the big bear in the air and descended slowly into the foggy depths of the birdhouse. Blizzard poked his head out of the velvet pouch and peered at the birds. He bared his teeth and growled again, as if to say, "Drop me and become my snack!"

"Holy smokes!" Richie called out. "Look at that! I don't—*eeeyaaahhh!*" Dodos seized him by the shoulders of his jacket and the cuffs of his jeans. They swept him up and lowered him into the abyss, belly first.

"Well," Noah said as he glanced at Ella, "who wants to go *neeexxxttt?*" He'd been snagged. "*Whooooaaa!*" he said as the dodos carried him down into the Forest of Flight.

Two more teams moved in for Ella and Podgy at the same time.

Noah felt as if he were skydiving. Though the height terrified him, he couldn't help noticing how spectacular the Forest of Flight was. A hundred shades of green, the forest was dotted with peculiar and variegated flowers. Thousands of birds coasted through the air, punching openings in leafy treetops and sailing beside waterfalls. Vines and ivy clung to everything, from the steel framework of the building to the trees and foliage.

"This is awesome!" Richie exclaimed, as if reading Noah's mind.

"*Waaa-hooo!*" cheered Ella.

Noah looked at them and smiled.

Like skydivers, the scouts extended their arms out to their sides. Even Podgy spread his flippers; he looked like an odd penguin superhero. Blizzard's black nose twitched as he sniffed the fresh air, and his dark eyes shone with excitement.

The earflaps of Noah's new cap snapped against his head. Adrenaline coursed through him from head to toe. This was a truly magical moment—one that he never could have imagined, not even in a dream. "We're coming, Megan!" he shouted. Each word was as sharp and distinct as a cracking whip.

Together the three children started to cheer. The dreamlike building came alive with a symphony of birds as chirps, squawks, and caws echoed in the vast space of the Forest of Flight. The noises drowned out every other sound. Birds sailed from branches and beams. They dived through the air, their swift movements a choreography danced to the music of their strange and wondrous voices.

✦ CHAPTER 37 ✦

THE MAN WHO ANSWERS QUESTIONS

The mist moistened Noah's cheeks as the dodos carried him down. The fog was so thick that he had to raise his hand to eye level just to glimpse his fingertips.

When the fog began to break apart, the crests of the trees and the walls of the birdhouse became visible again. Finally the ground of the Forest of Flight came into view. It was grassy and covered with rocks and streams and idle birds. The air was heavy with the smell of rich, pure dirt, so fertile that even an accidental seed could take root.

The dodos set the Action Scouts on the ground. They

unwrapped the velvet curtain they'd used to carry Blizzard, and all the birds flew into the trees except one, which stood on his pencil-thin legs and glanced about as if he expected something. With his large hooked bill and minuscule wings, he looked every bit the dodo that he was regrettably named.

"What do you suppose he wants?" Ella asked.

"I don't know. Maybe he's sticking around to help us," Noah said.

"To help us?"

"Maybe to show us around. This *is* his house, you know." Noah stepped up to the dodo. "Do you have a name?"

Ella paused before she said, "I hope you're not actually waiting for an answer."

"I wonder if he even has a name—something better than dodo," Noah said.

Without warning, they heard a rough, gravelly voice behind them. "You brats don't need to worry about names."

It was Charlie Red, surrounded by a new squad of police-monkeys. He snarled. Noah watched his lips peel off his teeth, half expecting to see fangs.

"Charlie! How did you—?" Noah's eyes darted toward the bamboo ramp, but all he could see was fog. "How did you get down here?"

Charlie Red and his monkey clan slid closer. He leaned forward and, as he spoke, dotted Noah's cheeks with spit.

"Let's just say I know the shortcuts."

To everyone's surprise, another voice erupted from behind Charlie. "You're not the only one who knows the shortcuts around here."

The voice came from a man with a head as big and round and hairless as a pumpkin and biceps the size of softballs.

"Tank!" Noah yelled.

Tank smiled and winked at Noah. "I see you checked your mailbox. And judging by those duds you're sportin', Podgy found you something to wear."

Furrowing his freckled brow, Charlie Red said, "Tank! What . . . ? What are you doing? I thought—"

"That was your first mistake," Tank said. He crossed his meaty arms over his chest. "Don't waste your time thinkin', bub."

"But . . . I thought . . . you—"

"It's over, Red," Tank said. "It's all over. They're Inside now. They know."

Suddenly a third voice rumbled behind Tank. "Indeed, it's all over!"

An old man stepped forward. He had thick gray hair tied in a ponytail and a bushy broom of a beard. Beaded sunglasses covered his eyes. A purple velvet trench coat draped his shoulders like a cloak. He turned to Charlie Red and said, "Charles, if you and your assistants will excuse us, I have much to speak about with our visitors."

Charlie, looking intimidated, nervous, and angry all at the same time, could only give in, saying, "Yes, Mr. Darby." Then, with a broad sweep of his arms, he led his flustered police-monkeys into the forest and out of sight.

The old man—Mr. Darby, as Charlie had called him—stood comfortably with his hands clasped behind his back.

"Ah yes," he said. "Blizzard and Podgy! I might have guessed the two of you would be in on this."

Mr. Darby's voice was warm and reassuring. He reached out and scratched Blizzard's cheek, just as one would scratch a kitten's chin. Blizzard closed his eyes halfway and droned a gentle growl. As a soft breeze wafted from the treetops, Marlo swept down and perched on Noah's shoulder.

"Well! Good day, Marlo," Mr. Darby said. The old man motioned to the dodo beside Noah. "Of course, Dodie is here, ready for whatever adventure may come his way."

"Dodie?" Ella asked.

"Yes," Mr. Darby said. "Dodie is this bird's name."

"Do all the animals have names?" Richie asked.

"Why, certainly! How else would we identify them?" He glanced at the massive branches that had fallen to the forest floor; they were completely entrenched in the earth. "You've certainly done your best to announce your arrival."

"Sorry about that," Noah said.

"The tree goons were chasing us," Ella piped up.

"Tree goons?" said Mr. Darby.

"Charlie Red's police-monkeys," Noah explained.

"Ah yes," Mr. Darby said. "Well, to Charles's credit, he and his band of monkeys work security, as does our friend Mr. Pangbourne, whom you know as Tank."

Tank shot the Action Scouts a wink and a smile.

"Well," Mr. Darby said as he stroked his messy gray beard, "allow me to formally introduce myself. I am Mr. Darby, and I am . . . well . . . let's say I'm the man who answers questions around here. I imagine the three of you must have some questions just about now."

"I can probably think of one or two," Ella said.

"Yeah—one or two *hundred*!" Richie corrected her.

Mr. Darby laughed. "I hardly think we have time for two hundred questions." He put one arm around Noah's shoulders and the other around Ella's and led the scouts along a path through the enormous trees. "But if all of you will join me, I think I'll be able to answer many of them."

Noah realized that he hadn't introduced himself. "Mr. Darby, I'm Noah. These are my friends—"

"Ella and Richie." Mr. Darby finished his sentence.

"Yes," Noah said. "How does everyone here know us?"

"Oh, the Action Scouts have been a topic of conversation around here for quite some time. Wouldn't you agree, Mr. Pangbourne?"

Tank smiled. His teeth looked like white jewels against his dark skin. "You ain't kiddin'."

"Mr. Darby," Ella said, "we don't even know where *here* is."

"Why, children," Mr. Darby replied, "you're in the Secret Zoo!"

CHAPTER 38

HUMMINGBIRD HIDEOUT

As Mr. Darby led the Action Scouts through the forest, he made no mention of the extraordinary building they were in. He said nothing about the birds circling overhead or about the police-monkeys and the impossibly tall trees. He casually led them along a winding path, whistling a tune that was quite merry.

The path stopped at a glass building that stood fifty feet high, a tiny edifice inside the Forest of Flight. Points of light reflected on the glass like stars. Mr. Darby opened a door and invited the scouts and their animal friends inside.

Like the Forest of Flight, the building was lush with

greenery—plants and trees that were shiny with dew. Little waterfalls splashed down rocky walls and spilled into narrow streams. Hummingbirds crowded the air. They darted back and forth and hovered in their magical flight. Occasionally they paused to drink honeysuckle nectar through their needle-fine beaks. Their wings thrummed over the flowers.

Mr. Darby swept his arm in a circle and said, "Welcome to Hummingbird Hideout!"

Marlo hopped off Noah's shoulder, soared into the trees, and darted back and forth. Watching him frolic with the hummingbirds, Noah wondered if he was excited to be the biggest bird in the sky for a change.

The scouts followed the old man and Tank along a flagstone path to a clearing, where pillowed chairs were arranged beside a marble fountain. In the center of the fountain was the statue of a hummingbird, so richly painted that the sprinkling water made it look soaked with blues and yellows and reds.

A dozen people dressed in green lab coats stood in a cluster. They were studying hummingbirds, poking flowers with thin steel probes, and scribbling busily on green notepads.

"Excuse me," Mr. Darby said to them. "I have business that requires a private meeting place. Might I use this area?"

One by one, the people in lab coats noticed the scouts, and their faces lit up. They agreed to Mr. Darby's request and hurried out of sight, whispering in one another's ears and casting curious glances back at Noah, Ella, and Richie.

"Please," Mr. Darby said as he motioned toward the chairs. "Take a seat."

Noah dropped onto the lush cushions, and they swallowed his rear end.

"How come it's like . . . like everyone here knows us?" he asked.

"A fair question," Mr. Darby said. He took a seat between Ella and Richie, who had sunk into their own fluffy chairs. "But it might be better to start by defining where *here* is, exactly."

"That will work for me," Ella said hastily.

Mr. Darby laughed, and his dark sunglasses slipped down his face. Before his eyes were revealed, he pushed them up again.

"You know, dear Ella, they've been saying you have a certain impatience about you."

"More like an appetite for new things," Ella said.

Mr. Darby laughed again. "I thought Richie was the one with the flashy vocabulary!"

"The flashy vocabulary *and* the flashy shoes," Ella quipped.

Richie corrected her. "Not anymore."

"Oh yeah! I forgot." Ella looked back at their host. "Richie was mugged by an ape. I guess the streets aren't safe even around here, Mr. Darby."

"Nothing has more potential for danger than the curiosity of an animal," Mr. Darby replied.

"Except maybe the curiosity of my sister," Noah cut in. "Do you know who she is, sir?"

Mr. Darby's face turned grave, and his features became sunken. "Megan," he said flatly.

The scouts bolted upright.

"You've seen her, then?" Noah asked.

"Not exactly."

"But she's okay, right?" Richie asked.

"I don't know."

"What do you mean?" Noah's voice trembled and his throat became dry.

Mr. Darby folded his hands in his lap. Hummingbirds buzzed around him. Three landed on his shoulders and softly pecked at his coat.

"There's so much to tell," he said. "Where shall I start?"

"How about the beginning?" Richie asked.

"Certainly," Mr. Darby said. He leaned forward, and a shadow fell across his face, making it so dark that he looked frightening. The hummingbirds whirled around him, their wings a fluttery blur. "But I must warn you.

The story is filled with such magic and sadness that few believe it."

Noah swept his hand around Hummingbird Hideout and said, "Sitting in this crazy place, I don't think you'll have a problem convincing us."

"Good," Mr. Darby said. He stroked his beard. "Then let's begin. Our story starts with a child, as so many stories do. The child's name was . . ."

CHAPTER 39

THE GOOD HEART
OF FREDERICK JACKSON

"Frederick Jackson," Mr. Darby said. "Frederick had warm eyes, a chubby face, and big freckles. He was sensitive and shy and very kind. In a way, it was Frederick Jackson's kindness that built the Secret Zoo.

"Frederick was raised mostly by his mother because his father was rarely home. You see, Frederick's father was a wealthy businessman. He owned several major construction companies, and he often traveled to distant cities. Though he loved his son dearly, his responsibilities kept them apart.

"One day when Frederick was nine years old—not much

younger than the three of you—his mother fell down the stairs in their house. His father was away on a business trip. His mother was hurt so badly that she couldn't move; she'd broken her legs and an arm, and she had other internal damage. Little Frederick was the only person who could help, but being so young and frightened, he didn't know what to do. He simply held his mother at the bottom of the stairs and screamed. By the time they were discovered, Frederick's mother had died."

"That's awful," Ella said.

"Indeed," Mr. Darby said. "So awful, in fact, that Frederick and Mr. Jackson sank into a deep depression. Mr. Jackson blamed himself for being away that day, and he secretly suspected that Frederick blamed him, too. Distance came between them. Over time, the distance grew. In order to be home with Frederick, Mr. Jackson stopped traveling with his construction crews. His businesses began to suffer. What little was left of the Jackson family was crumbling.

"Frederick turned ten and then eleven. The distance increased between the father and son. One afternoon, nearly three years after Frederick's mother had died, Mr. Jackson took his son on a hike through the countryside. They came upon a barn, where they were greeted by a farmer. The farmer tipped his straw hat and asked Mr. Jackson if he and his son would care to adopt a special pet. The farmer was selling his farm, and he couldn't take his pet with him. The animal was a langur."

Noah glanced at Richie and said, "A langur—like Mr. Tall Tail."

"That's right, Noah. Now Frederick's father was a sensible man." Mr. Darby continued. "He had no desire for a pet. But when Frederick caught sight of the langur leaping in the barn, he, for one reason or another, instantly fell in love with the critter. Frederick smiled. That was his first smile in three years. Mr. Jackson's heart swelled when he saw the joy on his son's face. The father was so touched that he took the animal home, no questions asked."

"What was the monkey's name?" Richie asked.

"Why, it was a grand name! Simon!" Mr. Darby trumpeted the monkey's name. "Simon the simian!"

"Oh, that's perfect!" Richie laughed.

"I don't get it," Ella admitted.

"A simian is a monkey," Richie explained. "Simon the simian! Get it? See how much more interesting life would be if you spent some time doing homework?"

Mr. Darby chuckled. As the hummingbirds whirled around him, their wings whirred their soothing hum. A few of the tiny birds perched on the old man's shoulders, thighs, and head; for an instant, one even touched down on his nose. None of this interfered with his storytelling.

"In no time, Frederick and Simon became best friends."

Mr. Darby continued. "The monkey restored happiness in the boy's heart, but unfortunately this miraculous feat came at a cost. You see, Simon proved to be a most discourteous houseguest. He had a fondness for shredding furniture, bashing china, and munching houseplants. He'd been in the Jackson home only a few months when Mr. Jackson decided that something must be done. But what? He couldn't send Simon away—not when the monkey was the only thing that made his son smile."

Mr. Darby paused. He seemed delighted to be sharing his tale, as if he were living it in the telling. He opened his palms, and three hummingbirds landed on them—splashes of color against his pale skin. The old man smiled and playfully tossed them in the air. He turned his attention back to the Action Scouts.

"Simon, you see, was the reason for the creation of the Clarksville City Zoo—your zoo."

"But how?" Ella asked.

"Mr. Jackson decided to build Simon the simian a special place to live. His construction crews built a massive steel cage for the langur on the lavish acres of his own property."

"How cool to have a construction crew at your disposal!" Richie blurted out.

"When the cage was built, Simon was moved into his

new home. An outdoor pet was unusual, indeed; even more unusual was a pet langur. News spread quickly, and before long, people lined up to peer over Mr. Jackson's fence for a look at Simon. Because Mr. Jackson was a generous man, he welcomed people onto his property for a closer look."

Noah said, "I think I know where this is going. Simon ends up becoming the first animal in the Clarksville City Zoo. Right?"

Mr. Darby raised his gray eyebrows above his sunglasses. "Precisely."

"Where did all the other animals come from?" Ella asked.

"Well, before long, a man showed up on Mr. Jackson's doorstep with an exotic pet, a white fox. He could no longer care for the fox, and he pleaded with Mr. Jackson to take it. Frederick loved the fox the moment he saw it, which made it impossible for Mr. Jackson to refuse the animal. Word spread that Mr. Jackson was adopting strange animals, and soon people came from near and far with their unwanted pets. Each new animal filled Frederick with such excitement that it was impossible for his father to turn any of them away. The private zoo grew and grew."

Mr. Darby paused to look affectionately at a green hummingbird perched on his finger.

"Hello, Speckle," he said. "How's my little friend doing today?"

The hummingbird rustled his feathers, tipped his head a few times, and dashed out of sight. At the same time, Tank arrived carrying a shiny tray crowded with tiny silver cups. He leaned forward and said, "Nectar, anyone?"

"We didn't notice that you'd left," Noah said.

"Mr. Darby tells a heck of a story, don't you think?" Tank replied.

He looked at Ella as he motioned to the tray.

"Nectar?" she asked. "From flowers?"

"Yep."

Ella twisted her face. "Gross!"

"You'll have to trust me on this one," Tank said. With two fingers, he pinched the handle of one cup and lifted it. The action seemed too delicate for his beefy hands. "Take a sip. This stuff is sweet enough to make soda taste like water."

Ella thought for a moment. Then she reluctantly took the cup and sipped gingerly from the brim. Her face lit up.

"Wow!" she exclaimed, and she gulped a mouthful. "You are the *man*, Tank!"

Tank offered the nectar to Noah and Richie, who suddenly looked anxious to try it. They snatched the cups from the tray and greedily sucked down the sweet juice.

"Now then," Mr. Darby said. "Where was I?"

"Strange animals were being parked on Mr. Jackson's doormat," Ella said.

"Yes. Thank you, Ella. Before long, the Jacksons had become the proud owners of twenty animals. Among them were four black-footed ferrets, a peacock, a crocodile, a chimpanzee, and a white tiger."

"He kept them in cages?" Noah asked. "All of them?"

"Yes. Each time a new animal arrived, Mr. Jackson put his construction crews to work."

"And people from all around kept coming to his house to see the animals?" Ella asked.

Mr. Darby laughed. "More and more came with every new animal. In fact, the private zoo became so well known that Mr. Jackson simply opened his property to the public and officially created the Clarksville City Zoo. With the opening of the zoo, Frederick was entirely relieved of his sadness. The animals had rescued him."

Noah said, "The zoo worked out well for everyone, then."

"I'm afraid not." Mr. Darby crossed his legs and straightened his purple trench coat. He pushed up his sunglasses and frowned. "For a while it did, yes. But something terrible happened—something so terrible that it is almost unspeakable."

Mr. Darby tried to say more, but his words were caught in his throat. The scouts waited apprehensively. After a long silence, the old man said, "Frederick died."

Richie gasped. "What? How?"

"No one knows. He died in his sleep, and the doctors weren't able to figure out why. It happened just weeks before his thirteenth birthday."

The scouts sat motionless, in silence, trying to make sense of the story.

"That's awful," Ella said at last.

Mr. Darby drew a deep breath and continued. "As you can imagine, Mr. Jackson did not take his son's death well. To lose his wife and son within the period of a few years not only broke the poor man's heart but also broke his mind."

"You mean he went crazy?" said Ella.

"Yes. It was a terrible thing. But ironically, it was his illness that helped create the Secret Zoo."

"Huh?" said Richie.

"The mind of a madman is a complicated thing. You see, the animals constantly reminded Mr. Jackson of Frederick. They were, after all, the creatures that had restored happiness in the boy's heart. Mr. Jackson couldn't look at them without seeing his son, and so he fell in love with them. He began to collect new ones. He opened global agencies that specialized in adopting exotic pets and wounded wild animals. He spent millions on their care and transport. Each new animal was kept in a cage on his property. All the townspeople realized that the poor man had gone mad, but given his plight, they understood why, and in a strange way, they loved him more because of his illness."

"What happened next?" Ella asked.

"His collection of animals grew. Five years after Frederick's death, Mr. Jackson had acquired over a hundred animals, but as his collection increased, so did his madness. Then, a couple of years later, his troubled mind shifted. His mental link between the animals and Frederick had become so strong that he believed he was keeping his own son captive. He couldn't bear that—not for an instant! There was only one thing for him to do."

Mr. Darby paused. He looked intently at the scouts, rose from his seat, and raised his hands up to the treetops. Hummingbirds filled the air, and the buzz of their wings resounded like strange music. Some fluttered down and perched along the old man's arms and shoulders.

"Mr. Jackson used the misfortune of his own life to create a glorious place. With old magic, simple ambition, and a pure heart, he created the most magnificent structure time has known." Mr. Darby cupped his hands together. "Mr. Jackson created the Secret Zoo."

CHAPTER 40

BHANU LAKSHMAN AND MR. DEGRAFF

"Magic . . ." Ella said in a soft, dreamy tone that made the word come out like a song. She aimed her glassy stare at the ceiling and seemed to consider the possibilities.

Richie was more direct in sharing his feelings: "Totally . . . totally . . . totally cool."

Mr. Darby fell into his seat with a sigh. Most of the hummingbirds settled back into the trees. Beside Noah, a green hummingbird paused to sip from a flower cup, hovering in the air as if suspended by invisible strings.

The scouts' animal friends were playing in the green underbrush. Blizzard was waving his head between giant flowers and burying his snout in pink petals. Dozens of hummingbirds had perched along his back. They looked like colorful bows in his thick white fur. At Blizzard's side was Podgy. A hummingbird had settled on his head, and he was waddling around, trying to shake it off. Above them, Dodie and Marlo swooped through the trees, chasing a rainbow-colored cluster of hummingbirds.

Mr. Darby combed his bushy gray beard with his fingers and continued his story where he had left off.

"He instructed his crews to construct something to replace the cages. Mr. Jackson wanted something more, and he—or his madness—insisted that there was a way. Unfortunately, no one had an idea that wasn't based on extending the walls of the cages. This was not good enough for Mr. Jackson.

"The crew leaders were baffled. No one could understand what Mr. Jackson wanted. Most of them believed that the poor man had completely lost his mind, and they tried to ignore him. But he would not give up. He knew he could do something. He just didn't know what it was. Three months later, Mr. Jackson finally found what he was searching for."

Mr. Darby reached into his purple trench coat and pulled out an old leather-bound book. "This is one of Mr. Jackson's diaries. It's normally kept in the Library of the Secret Society, but—"

"The Secret Society?" Noah interrupted. "What's that?"

"The Secret Society? Why, that's us! Tank, myself, Blizzard, Podgy, Dodie, Marlo, every hummingbird in Hummingbird Hideout, and many people and animals that you have yet to meet." Mr. Darby paused. Then he added, "Perhaps the three of you are part of the Secret Society now, too."

"Us?" Richie said. "Secret Society?"

"Coooool!" said Ella.

"Fate has selected you," Mr. Darby said. Ella tried to speak, but Mr. Darby held up his palm to stop her. "Let me continue."

The old man opened his book and began to read. "I was home alone. When I heard the knock . . ."

I was home alone. When I heard the knock, I crossed the foyer and opened the front door. Standing on the porch was a pale young man. At first glance, I actually believed him to be a ghost—a man of spirit, dead many years, and no longer a body of flesh and blood. I feared the worst. I feared that I had died and that this creature was here to guide me to the world beyond.

After standing in shock for a moment, I asked, "What do you want?"

The peculiar man slid his wet hands together and said, "A minute of your time."

Though he was terribly strange, I couldn't let him stand

on the porch in the cold rain. I showed him indoors.

I made a pot of tea, and we sat down in my study. After some time, the man said, "My name is Mr. DeGraff," and he held out his hand. His skin was sickly yellow; his nails were like claws. With great reluctance, I shook his hand.

Mr. DeGraff stood and wandered to a bookshelf. He stroked the bindings with his ugly fingers, reading the titles as he moved.

"Do you enjoy reading, Mr. DeGraff?" I asked.

"Not at all," he answered, keeping his eyes fixed on the books. "I hate reading. Words bore me. They're petty and sad. I'm a man of action." Then he changed the topic. "I understand you have . . . oh, about a hundred and seventeen pets that you don't know what to do with."

I was about to reply, but Mr. DeGraff spoke first. "But I know, Mr. Jackson! I know what to do with them."

I couldn't help being intrigued.

"Explain yourself," I said. "But do so quickly, because this conversation is growing foolish."

Mr. DeGraff would not be rushed. He continued to slither along the bookshelves, dragging his pallid finger across the spines. When he spoke again, it was only to say, "I'll talk when I'm ready to talk."

I felt my face flush with anger. I pointed toward the door and shouted, "Mr. DeGraff, you are invited to leave, sir!"

Unbothered, Mr. DeGraff shrugged and glided toward the door, saying, "I'm sorry—sorry for you, that is."

I couldn't restrain my curiosity. I grabbed hold of the strange man and said, "You have two minutes. Two minutes! If you cannot figure out what you want to say by then, I'll happily return you to the storm!"

Mr. DeGraff smiled a black, nearly toothless grin. He walked back into the room and said, "I know a way that you can return your pets to the wild without . . . well . . . without returning them to the wild."

"And how is that?"

"You simply increase their space. That's all 'the wild' is anyway—space."

I laughed and said, "That's it? That's how you can solve my problems?"

"No," Mr. DeGraff said. He buried his fingers in his pocket and pulled out a wrinkled slip of paper. He looked deeply in my eyes, as if trying to communicate with his own. "This . . . ," he said, "this is how I can solve your problems."

I snatched the paper and read it. On it was a name, Bhanu Lakshman, and below that, the name of a city in India.

"This man," Mr. DeGraff said, "was born under exceptional circumstances, and as a result, he can accomplish exceptional things. Some claim that he is skilled in magic. He is the one you need to see."

"What? You're insane!" I declared.

But Mr. DeGraff was done with the conversation. He was already on his way to the front door.

"This is ludicrous!" I shouted. "You come here with stories of magic and—"

Mr. DeGraff wrapped his yellow fingers around the doorknob and stopped. Without looking back, he flatly stated, "Mr. Jackson, our time together has come to an end." The strange man stepped out the door and crept into the dark, rainy night.

I stood in the empty foyer and read the name a second time: Bhanu Lakshman.

"Wait a minute!" I roared. "Mr. DeGraff!"

I ran to the door and threw it open, but the man was gone. It was as if he'd been taken by the night.

Taken, in fact, by the shadows . . .

Mr. Darby paused.

Ella asked, "Did Mr. Jackson go to India?"

"Yes," Mr. Darby said. "He did."

"And he found Bhanu?"

"It took some time—some seeking—but he did find Bhanu."

"Then what happened?"

Mr. Darby resituated his sunglasses on his nose and continued to read. "After several months, I discovered Bhanu . . ."

After several months, I discovered Bhanu Lakshman in North India. He had kind dark eyes, neatly clipped hair, and flowing

Indian garb. He carried his chin high, his shoulders back. I explained that I had traveled a long way and wanted only a moment of his time. Bhanu agreed, and I told my story. Bhanu sat and listened, occasionally sipping his tea but saying nothing. As I spoke, his penetrating stare seemed to look inside me more than upon me.

When I finished, he asked, "And what, my friend, do you expect of me?"

"I've traveled a long way. Someone—a person I don't know—said you have supernatural talents . . . magical abilities. He said you could help me create something for the animals."

Bhanu smiled. "With all your money and machines, you cannot create something yourself?"

"No, I cannot," I said.

Bhanu said, "India is my home, my friend. America lies a great distance from my home."

He paused and faced me squarely. His stare was piercing. It was as if he could see something in my eyes—my past, my pain, my hope.

After a long time, he said, "Perhaps I can do . . . things. But there are limits to my gifts. You should know this before we begin. You should also know that I will need my brothers. Without them—without our physical bond—there are no . . . 'magical abilities,' as you said."

"Your brothers?" I asked.

"Yes. I have two identical brothers. They will have to join

me in my adventure to America. They will be needed."

"You . . . you're one of three?"

"Yes, triplets. But we were not born of the same mother."

"What?"

"Kavi, Vishal, and I were born of different mothers in different cities."

"That's impossible!"

"What is more remarkable is that my brothers and I were born at exactly the same moment, weighing exactly the same amount, and measuring exactly the same length. And our mothers all bore the same name—Kavita."

I was too stunned and confused to speak.

"We will help you, Mr. Jackson. We will help you, because I believe the work of the gods has brought us together, across such a vast distance, so that I may help you . . . and you may help me."

"Help you? Help you how?"

"I'm afraid I must attach to my offering one condition."

"Go ahead."

Bhanu told me. I quickly agreed.

ఆ౿ CHAPTER 41 ౿ఢ

Magic and Machines

Hummingbirds continued to buzz around Mr. Darby; they landed on him as if he were a statue in a fountain. He closed the diary, set it aside, and said to the scouts, "The four men left for America the following week."

"But what did Bhanu want?" Richie asked. "He said he wanted something. What was it?"

The old man looked into space and contemplated something. A minute later, he said, "I don't know how to say this without just saying it. I've told you of the Secret Society; now let me explain it. The Secret Society is a band of humans and animals that has existed since the dawn of the first day. It is devoted to protecting animals, especially those that are threatened by humankind."

"Those in danger of extinction?" Ella asked.

"Yes," Mr. Darby said.

"Hold on!" Noah said. "This explains the dodo birds. You guys saved them from dying off. Right?"

"Yes," Mr. Darby said. "Hundreds of years ago, a Dutch sailor—one of *us*—saw what was happening to the dodos. He rescued several and hid them in a secluded part of the island that the ship had landed on. Weeks later, he managed to escape with the birds. Thus he rescued the species."

"But the Secret Zoo wasn't built until many years later," Ella pointed out. "How did he protect the dodos for that long?"

"Though the Secret Society once operated in isolated groups, the members were very effective. The Earth has ways to conceal the truth, and the Secret Society found them. Caverns, forests, mountains, and deserts—each has a bounty of hiding places.

"The independent groups of the Secret Society grew larger and larger. Concerns about their geographic separation began to surface. Bhanu happened to be a member of the Secret Society, and what he wanted in exchange for helping Mr. Jackson was a place where everyone could come together in an organized fashion. This place would also ensure the safety of the animals."

"So Bhanu and his brothers built the Secret Zoo?" Noah asked.

"Yes, but not without help."

"Help?"

"The help of Mr. Jackson. But more important than that, the help of his construction crews. Together, using magic and machines, they dug into the earth and opened the sky."

Richie's mouth dropped, and Ella's eyes widened.

"I don't get it," Noah said.

"Mr. Jackson's construction crews tunneled into the ground. As they did so, Bhanu and his brothers gave light and air and sky and stars to the caverns. Bhanu and his brothers put the elements of the world into the holes and tunnels."

"But I saw Arctic Town," Noah said. "That's no simple hole in the ground. It's enormous! I mean, look at how big this birdhouse is!"

"The brothers could expand space. They could take a hole and make it a thousand times its size."

"But first they needed the hole!" Ella called out. "That's where the construction guys came in! The larger the hole, the larger the space the brothers could create!"

"Something like that," Mr. Darby said. He scratched

his unkempt gray beard and added, "But it was more difficult than that."

"How?" Noah asked.

Mr. Darby said, "Let's go for a walk. Some fresh air will
help us. Besides," the old man added with a smile, "we
have urgent business to tend to."

❧ CHAPTER 42 ❧

BACK AT THE CITY OF SPECIES

Mr. Darby led them through Hummingbird Hideout and across the Forest of Flight. They crossed a bridge over a river, and that led them to a small island in the middle of the water. On the island was a giant elevator made of glass—the walls, the floor, and the ceiling. Attached to the outside of the floor and ceiling were the mechanics—gears, pulleys, cables, and other unnameable pieces. Mr. Darby, the scouts, Tank, and the animals were able to fit inside.

As the elevator ascended into the fog, Ella asked, "Is this thing . . . *magic?*"

"Not at all," Mr. Darby replied. "This elevator was built about fifty years ago by a brilliant young team of engineers—kids not much older than you, in fact."

Noah observed the view as they climbed through the monstrous tree limbs. "Where are they now?"

Tank answered this time. "Most of them are retired and live in Senior City."

"Where's that?" Richie said.

"On the outskirts of the City of Species," Tank said. His deep voice boomed and echoed off the elevator walls. "It's a little place—more like a town than a city. Most of us live here in the City of Species."

"How many people are in the Secret Society?" Ella asked.

Tank looked at Mr. Darby and said, "How many are we now? A thousand?"

"Nine hundred and fifty-two, the last time I checked," said Mr. Darby.

"Nine hundred and fifty-two!" Noah gasped. "And they all live here?"

"Most of them do," Mr. Darby said. "Some are Crossers."

"Crossers?" Noah asked.

"Those who cross between the Secret Zoo and the outside world. Some of them even have lives on the Outside."

The elevator climbed through the fog and into the open space above, where the scouts saw a host of birds. Many of them chased the glass box and flew circles around it. Some perched on the roof, hitching a ride into the heights of the Forest of Flight. To Noah it seemed that the birds were happy—happy that Mr. Darby had found the Action Scouts.

The elevator stopped beside an enormous branch. It shifted upward and crossed the branch as giant gears and pulleys worked the cables. It snapped into place between thick rails built between the tree limbs; they reminded Noah of rails he'd seen in subway stations. From there, the elevator rocketed ahead, breaking twigs and frightening birds into the air, and stopped at a narrow, dark hallway built into the wall of the Forest of Flight. The elevator door opened, the group exited, and at the end of the hallway, Mr. Darby flung open a velvet curtain, revealing the city.

With a sweep of his arms, the old man said, "Here we are! Back in the City of Species!"

The scouts ducked beneath a waterfall and hopped over a stream to reach the city streets, which were still packed with animals. A panda bear pranced up to Ella.

"Hey, big fella," she said.

The panda playfully nudged its head against her and scampered off.

"See that, Richie?" Ella said. "You're not the only popular person around here."

"Speaking of that," Richie said as he pointed across the road, "look who's coming."

A small band of prairie dogs charged across the street, headed straight for Richie. They scurried around his feet in circles and stared at his heels. Richie tiptoed through the jittery little herd, trying not to squash any of them.

Mr. Darby noticed the commotion and bellowed an encouraging laugh. "I see you have even more companions, yes?"

One of the prairie dogs, a chubby critter with a face as round and large as a softball, had taken a special liking to Richie. He bounced at his side, staring up at him.

"What's the deal with this one?" Richie asked.

"That's P-Dog," Tank said.

"P-Dog?" Richie said. "Let me guess. The *p* stands for 'Prairie.'"

"They all have names, right?" Ella asked. "Like the hummingbirds."

"Yep," Tank said. "That's P-Dog, and over there is Hot Dog, and . . . let me see . . . that's Chili Dog and Nibbles and Dog Tag."

"Mr. Darby," Richie said, "can all the animals at the City Zoo get to the Secret Zoo? You know, the way the prairie dogs did?"

"Absolutely."

"But how is that possible?"

"Through a hundred years of magic and machines. We never stop building. We never stop imagining. And we never stop creating. Bhanu's magic is still alive in the Secret Zoo, and we never stop using it."

Richie said, "The sectors . . . all the doorways with those velvet curtains . . . I don't see how—"

"Each sector has a habitat that's suitable for any number of species. All the cages in the City Zoo have a passage to at least one sector, and every sector has a passage to the City of Species. From what I've heard, Noah came through a sector via a passage from Penguin Palace. You and Ella came through a sector that's connected to Little Dogs of the Prairie."

Ella said, "You mean all the exhibits at the zoo are connected to this place?"

"Yes. On top of that, many exhibits at the City Zoo even have secret access into the outside world."

"That's how Blizzard got into the tunnel," Richie said. "But why do they need access to the outside world?"

"They patrol."

"They *what*?"

"They patrol. They protect the Secret Zoo and its perimeter."

Noah said, "That explains the monkeys that Megan saw on the rooftops in our neighborhood."

Richie said, "But what are they patrolling for?"

Mr. Darby looked at the sky and combed his fingers through his beard for several moments. Then he turned his eyes back to Richie.

"I think that conversation will be best saved for later."

More and more animals gathered in the City of Species. They were pushing through the sector curtains and piling into the streets.

"What's going on?" Noah asked.

"You're about to see," Mr. Darby said. The old man paused and added, "Now is the time to tell you what we know about Megan. But I must warn you that the story might be difficult to hear."

"We can take it," Ella assured him.

An ostrich stopped to peck at something in the street. Ella jumped to dodge its fat feathered rump.

Mr. Darby stopped walking and faced the scouts. "Some of us think Megan might be trapped—trapped in a secured area called the Dark Lands."

"The Dark Lands?" Ella said.

"The Dark Lands are a bad place. They are filled with animals—wretched things called sasquatches. Some believe the sasquatches . . ." Mr. Darby paused as if he didn't want to speak his next words. "Some believe they have trapped Megan."

The warmth drained from Noah's cheeks. He glanced at Ella. She looked strange, almost unreal, like a mannequin that had been made up to look like Ella.

"Trapped?" he whispered.

"Yes. If she is indeed trapped in the Dark Lands, the only way to free her is by entering that murky region." Mr. Darby paused and clasped his hands together. "And doing that would likely be . . . well, doing that would likely be the greatest trial the Secret Zoo has ever attempted."

CHAPTER 43

More Secrets of the Secret Zoo

"Are you certain?" Noah asked. "Are you certain she's in there?"

"No, Noah, I'm afraid not." Mr. Darby straightened his beaded sunglasses. "I need to show you something. Follow me. As we walk, I'll tell you what we know."

"Start with the sasquatches," Ella said as they headed down the street. "What are they?"

"Creatures trapped between humankind and animal-kind. Part human and part ape, they embody the worst of man and the worst of animal. Sasquatches once existed in the outside world—your world."

"Wait a minute! Are you talking about Bigfoot?"

"Sasquatches have been called many names."

"But Bigfoot's not real," Ella said. "He's a myth."

"Bigfoot may be a myth, but the sasquatches are real, I assure you. They once existed in small numbers in the outside world. They remained hidden to protect their species and lived in vastly different regions of the earth—Antarctica, the Himalayas, even the jungles of South America. Sasquatches adapt easily to different climates, and they are good at survival. Over the course of history, however, their isolation caused their numbers to diminish, almost to the point of extinction. That is why eighty-seven years ago, the Secret Society began a two-year expedition to locate as many sasquatches as possible. We were able to track down nearly three dozen. We brought them here—that was no easy feat, mind you—to guard them from extinction."

"What happened?" Richie asked. "I mean, things obviously turned bad."

"'What happened' is well documented in many texts lining the shelves in the Library of the Secret Society. I've read them all. With an aim toward brevity, I'll spare you most of the details now."

Richie nodded, and the scouts silently waited for more.

"The sasquatches were unruly. Within days, they escaped into isolated parts of random sectors. We decided to give the sasquatches the isolation they preferred. They are truly creatures of the shadows."

Richie said, "That's why we never see them in our world—the Outside."

"Yes . . . though I'm not sure they even exist in the Outside any longer. We monitor sasquatch activity, and we haven't had a real sighting in thirty years."

"What happened after that?"

"For years, the sasquatches hid in the sectors. Just when many of us in the Secret Society thought they'd died off, they were spotted. Some considered this good news— we thought they might be ready to join our society. We were terribly wrong. One night, the sasquatches stormed the City of Species and attacked us. Hundreds of our members perished that night, animals and people alike. Countless buildings were destroyed. It was the Secret Zoo's darkest moment."

"What did you do?" Ella asked.

"The inevitable. We fought back. We pushed them out of the city and drove them into a single sector."

As Mr. Darby finished his sentence, the group came to a wall covered by velvet curtains. The old man touched the folds, sending a ripple across them.

"This is the sector. This, I'm afraid, is where we barricaded the sasquatches. This is the entrance to the Dark Lands."

Noah inspected the curtains. Once upon a time, they had been white, but now they were stained yellow and dotted with ugly brown spots. Some of the fabric was matted; several patches were flimsy and almost threadbare. The curtains seemed to be decaying, as if the badness of the Dark Lands were rotting them away. Noah peered behind the folds. The wall was made of ordinary bricks.

"Bricks hold them back?" Noah asked.

"The magic of the curtains is what binds the bricks and seals the Dark Lands."

"But what about the other passage?" Richie asked. "The passage that leads to our world?"

"The sector used to open at the elephant exhibit, but we closed it off."

"That doesn't make sense," Noah said. "If the Dark Lands are sealed off, how did Megan get in?"

"Well, it's difficult for humans to travel between the City Zoo and the Secret Zoo. The portals between the sectors and the zoo exhibits are designed for animals, not humans. Our Crossers have had a dreadful time traveling back and forth. The night your sister disappeared, she was spotted in Creepy Critters. Do you know the Chamber of Lights?"

The scouts nodded.

"It's one of our new projects. The Chamber of Lights is

still under construction, and it's in an early testing phase. It's meant to be a quick gateway from the City Zoo to any sector of the Secret Zoo. At this point, it's not reliable. It's not even safe.

"Anyway, somehow Megan discovered the magic of the Chamber of Lights, and she used it to cross into the Secret Zoo. The frogs found three pages of her journal inside the chamber—the three pages that the animals secretly delivered to you. Though we believe Megan made it inside the Secret Zoo, we've never been able to locate her. This is precisely why many think she crossed into the Dark Lands. You see, if the Chamber of Lights isn't used correctly, any sector of the Secret Zoo could be at the other end of the crossing."

"Why didn't you tell my family about this?" Noah asked. "You should have told us!"

"Many of us wanted to, but that would have meant exposing our secrets. It would have been too dangerous for us—too dangerous for the world."

"Why the world?" Ella asked. "Tank said the same thing, and I—"

Mr. Darby interrupted her. "There is a man. A man who walks in the shadows, who literally draws breath from the shadows. Some claim he's a myth, a legend. But I believe he is trying to get into our Secret Zoo, trying to get near the source of our power and magic. And I believe that if he gets to it . . ." Mr. Darby looked at the ground and stroked his scraggly beard. "I can't even think of it."

"But what is he—?" Ella could barely contain herself.

Mr. Darby raised his hand sharply and said, "That's enough about him for now! It chills me to the bone even to think of him. Besides, he is a subject best left for another time—a time when there *is* more time."

Noah brought the subject back to Megan. "But you only *think* Megan's inside the Dark Lands. You're not sure."

"Yes. That's the main reason that the Secret Society hasn't gone in after her. If we bring down this wall, the sasquatches might escape—that is, if the sasquatches are even in there. More than eighty years have passed since we last saw them, and we're not sure whether they have survived. We are uncertain about so many things. Uncertainty is the reason that we've done nothing."

"That's crazy!" Noah cried. "You can't just give up on Megan!"

"No one has given up. Since her disappearance, endless thoughts and discussions have been about Megan. Many members of our society will be relieved that the Gifteds found a way to involve the three of you."

"The *who*?" Ella asked. "Gifteds—who are they?"

"Animals that seem, in some regards, almost human. Greater intelligence, awareness, compassion—higher evolutionary characteristics, I suppose you could say. You've met a few already. Blizzard, Marlo, Little Bighorn—some of our brightest. In our world, they're natural leaders, often bridging the gap between us and the animals. It's hard to imagine where we'd be without them."

Ella said, "But *all* the animals seem smart."

Mr. Darby nodded. "Most are, yes. It so happens that some are more capable than others."

"What changed them?" Richie asked. "The magic?"

"In part," Mr. Darby said. "But some think they're advancing because we treat them as equals."

Noah didn't care about the Gifteds. He cared about Megan, and he shifted the conversation back to her. "We need to get inside the Dark Lands! There may be only a slight chance that Megan's in there, but we need to find out for sure."

"I believe you're right," Mr. Darby said. "And now that the three of you are here, the members of the Secret Council have called an emergency meeting to plot a course of action. That's where all these animals are headed, and that's where we need to be." Mr. Darby turned abruptly into a winding alley. As he passed between a tower and a giant moss-covered tree, he said, "Come! Follow me, Action Scouts. We don't want to be late."

"Late for what?" Ella called as they raced after the old man.

Without looking back, Mr. Darby replied, "You'll see, Ella. You'll see."

As they headed down the alley, they heard an indistinct rumble. With each step forward, the noise grew louder until it engulfed and overwhelmed them.

◆❧ CHAPTER 44 ❧◆

THE SCOUTS TAKE CENTER STAGE

When the scouts stepped out of the alley, they found themselves on the other side of the city. The area was so packed with animals that moving forward was difficult. Animals filled the streets, the sidewalks, the alleyways—they were everywhere. Monkeys swung from tree limbs, dangled from balconies, and rode on other animals. Reptiles clung to the sides of buildings. Birds were perched on trees, rooftops, awnings, and electrical wires.

When the animals saw the scouts, they moved aside; some squirmed, some flew, and some hopped to allow them passage. The path led to a low wooden stage, where a group of people wearing trench coats sat in wide, pil-lowed chairs. The Secret Council. Noah found it inter-esting that Mr. Darby was the only member whose coat was made of velvet. Animals affectionately moved across the Secret Council—monkeys jumped across their laps, snakes slithered across their shoes, and lizards climbed up their backs—but the council members barely seemed to notice.

Mr. Darby's beard danced as he turned to face his guests. "Come! Come!" he said, and he stepped onto the path.

The three children advanced slowly through the crowd. Excited by their arrival, the animals erupted in a commo-tion, flapping their wings, stomping their paws, and clomp-ing their hooves. Grunts and screeches echoed across the City of Species. The noise was deafening. Continuously waving to greet the crowd, Mr. Darby led the scouts and their animal friends to the stage. They climbed up and strode to the middle of the Secret Council, settled in their seats of honor.

Mr. Darby turned toward the spectacular congregation, and an eerie quiet washed over the streets. He cleared his throat.

"Esteemed members of our Secret Council and members of our Secret Society! As most of you undoubtedly know, today we have unexpected visitors in our city—extremely important visitors. I have called this emergency session of the council to hear your voice in the matter of the Megan Situation. But first, let me say a few words."

For fifteen minutes, Mr. Darby reviewed the Megan Situation, including the facts about her disappearance, the theories regarding her whereabouts, the likelihood of saving her, and the possible dangers in attempting a rescue. From start to finish, the Action Scouts gazed at the dreamlike crowd of animals and people. At the end of his speech, Mr. Darby said, "Does anyone wish to ask questions or make statements?"

An enormous man with a stomach as round as a beach ball pushed to the front of the crowd and threw himself against the stage. "I'd like to hear from the boy."

"The boy?" said Mr. Darby.

"That one," the man said. He shook his oversized finger up at Noah. It looked like a trembling hot dog. "The one who claims relation to the girl!"

Mr. Darby leaned close to Noah and grinned. "Are you the one who 'claims relation to the girl'?" he whispered.

Too frightened to speak, Noah simply looked at Mr. Darby.

Mr. Darby stepped aside to give Noah and the huge man a clear view of each other. A hush fell over the City of Species.

The man stuffed his big fingers into his pockets and said, "Young man, do you understand how dangerous it is for you to be here?"

"I . . . I think so," Noah replied.

"Do you understand what your presence means?" he asked. "Do you understand what your sister has done? Do you realize how she has divided this great society?" The man's voice rumbled.

"Yes. I think Mr. Darby explained—"

"You think your sister is in the Dark Lands? What proof do you have? We need proof!" he demanded.

Noah caught sight of Blizzard on the stage. Noah wasn't the only one who didn't like the way this man was acting. The polar bear looked ready to lunge at the man and take a healthy bite out of his rear end.

"I . . . I don't have any proof, sir. But the animals found her notes and—"

"You don't have proof? You don't have proof, and yet you stand here before me—before all of us in the City of Species—and ask us to open our homeland, our haven and shelter, to the threat of the Dark Lands?"

"I . . . I guess so. I mean . . . No!" Noah paused for a moment and added, "I mean . . . I don't know."

"You don't know?" The man shook his head disapprovingly. "You *don't know*!"

Noah stood dumbfounded, clenching his hands. He felt dreadfully small and insignificant.

The man turned toward the Secret Council. "This young man would like us to open our community—our homes, our streets, and our schools—to the dangers of the Dark Lands. Why? Because he has a hunch that his sister might be in there!"

Noah had no idea of what to say. Tears welled up in his eyes.

Ella jumped forward and shouted, "Watch it, tubby! Don't you talk to my friend like that!" Her ponytail and the fluffy mounds of her earmuffs bounced on her head.

"Young lady!" the man said. "When you—"

"I'm still talking!" Ella interrupted. "Do you know who we are? We're the Action Scouts. Nobody talks to us like that!"

"The Action Scouts!" the man said mockingly. "Why, of course. We're dealing with the Action Scouts. Why, I'd simply forgotten!" He shrugged his shoulders and rolled his eyes. Nervous chuckles rippled through the council.

"Don't you—"

Noah took Ella's arm, and their eyes met for a moment. Feeding off Ella's support, Noah found himself taking three steps toward the man.

"If Megan's not in the Dark Lands, then where is she? The animals in Creepy Critters—they saw her go into the Chamber of Lights and then disappear. Mr. Darby told us so! If you can't find her anywhere in the Secret Zoo, then where else can she be?"

THE SCOUTS TAKE CENTER STAGE 237

The man raised one eyebrow and grimaced. He knew Noah had a good point.

"She's in the Dark Lands, and you know it! You're just afraid of what that means."

The man parted his lips to say something, but Noah went on before he could speak.

"My sister's gone!" he cried. "Do you understand what that's done to *my* home? To *my* community? Do you know how many people—people I've never even met—have been crushed by her disappearance? I'm not trying to put anyone in danger. Not at all! I'm only asking the Secret Society to help me find my sister. Help me bring her home." Noah paused. He searched for some powerful words to influence the crowd, but he could think of none. What came out instead was the simple truth. "I . . . I miss her."

A hush swept across the council. The crowd became still. Even the monkeys stopped chattering.

Mr. Darby touched the boy's shoulder and said, "Thank you, Noah." He turned back to the enormous congregation. "I believe now would be a good time to put this to a vote. All those in favor of opening the Dark Lands, let us hear from you."

The city erupted with noise and commotion. Chimpanzees screeched and swung through the trees. Birds squawked and flew through the air. Elephants trumpeted and pounded their feet. Alligators hissed and clanked their tails against signposts. Near the stage, a giraffe hoisted its long neck into the air with three prairie dogs on its head so their squeaky barks could be heard. Ella and Richie ran to Noah and hugged him.

When the clamor faded, Mr. Darby turned to the people seated onstage and said, "And who in the Secret Council is in favor of advancing into the Dark Lands?"

Everyone onstage raised a hand.

"Well, Action Scouts," Mr. Darby said, "I think the decision has been made."

The scouts cheered and exchanged high fives.

"Give me one hour to finalize the logistics of Operation Wrecking Crew and Rescue," Mr. Darby said as he walked past the council to leave the stage.

"Operation Wrecking Crew and Rescue?" exclaimed a council member. "We never discussed such a plan."

"Who said the council would discuss it?" Mr. Darby called out. "One must occasionally think for oneself, yes?" He directed his gaze intently at the scouts and said, "By the way, there's one thing I want the three of you to know—to *really* understand."

"Yes?" said Ella.

"Even if Megan is in the Dark Lands, there's no guarantee that we'll bring her out. You understand this, right?"

The scouts nodded.

"You should also know," he warned, "that we ourselves might never make it out of there. You need to truly understand this. If the sasquatches have survived, there's a formidable chance that many of us will not."

The scouts huddled together, and for the first time, they looked afraid. Then they all nodded at once.

"Good." Mr. Darby spun around. "Let us not waste any more time. I'll round up my crew."

"Your crew?" the scouts chimed.

"You'll see, scouts," Mr. Darby said. "You'll see."

CHAPTER 45

OPERATION WRECKING CREW AND RESCUE

During the next hour, the animals evacuated the area in front of the bricked entrance to the Dark Lands. Into the clearing stepped a small group of elephants, polar bears, and rhinos. They stood side by side, two hundred feet from the curtain. Behind them, the city was alive in a hullabaloo: birds and monkeys leaping across tree-tops, possums swinging from balconies, and otters and penguins swimming up and down streams. Everyone was nervous.

The scouts stood under a large tree, watching the operation unfold. A group of concerned Secret Cityzens walked up and offered them snacks that were just short of a full meal. The scouts gratefully accepted—they were starving. They quickly devoured everything: apples, bananas, berry-filled granola bars, chocolate, and warm homemade bread soaked in rich butter. They sucked down tall glasses of cold water and tiny cups of sweet nectar.

As they cleaned up from their snack, Noah realized he had no idea what time it was. It seemed as if the scouts had been in the Secret Zoo for days, but surely it had been nothing more than a few hours. He asked Richie, who checked his watch and reported the time as just past four in the morning. Noah was right: barely four hours had passed since his adventure first began with a cheetah arriving at his mailbox.

Five additional elephants stepped through the crowd and into the clearing. Each had lugged a wooden cart filled with monstrous boulders. Two of the rhinos briefly stepped out of the line to lift the front ends of the carts, dumping the boulders to the ground. Each boulder was no less than seven feet high and wrapped in steel mesh. Dozens of monkeys scurried up nearby trees with steel cables pinched in their teeth. All at once, they dropped the cables over the strongest available branches. On the ground, several men ran back and forth, collecting the cables and harnessing one end to an elephant and the other to a boulder. When that was done, the elephants backed up, raising the boulders in the air with ho-hum ease. Two lions stepped forward and pulled back the curtains. In an emergency, the boulders and curtains could be dropped instantly to close off the Dark Lands once again. The elephants would hold up the boulders as long as the operation was in progress.

Noah pointed to one of the animals in the line. "There's Blizzard!" he shouted, and he charged into the street, calling, "C'mon, guys!"

When the scouts reached Blizzard, the big polar bear rolled his head and let them wrap him in their arms.

Richie darted to the rhinos at one end of the line, calling out, "Ella, look who's here!"

"Little Bighorn!" Ella screamed. She rushed over and stroked the rhino's head. "How did I know we'd be seeing you again?"

"Everyone! Can I have your attention please?" Mr. Darby was standing on a hippo the size of a small car, talking into a megaphone. His voice rose above the hubbub. "This day has been waiting for us. We are about to embark on a great and possibly dangerous adventure. It is only fitting that we are joined by three children known as the Action Scouts." Mr. Darby winked at the scouts. "We have had long debates on how to handle the Megan Situation. Today, my friends, we have closed those debates and are determined to take action!"

The scouts cheered along with the rest of the crowd.

"Now, let us go forward without fear or hesitation. Let us march into the Dark Lands and do what we can to bring a lost girl home."

Animals growled and paced back and forth. Birds flew out of trees and soared in the sky. People shouted. The air grew thick with tension.

Mr. Darby pointed to the Dark Lands and turned to the small group of animals at the front. His voice blasted through the megaphone as he said, "Let's bring that wall down!"

In unison, the enormous animals huffed and snorted. A moment later, they were off, headed toward the brick wall with terrifying power. Their footfalls rumbled and echoed off the buildings. The scouts ran to Mr. Darby, who was still standing on the hippo's back. Noah thought he looked like an old soldier rallying his troops from the top of an army tank.

"Mr. Darby!" Ella called out.

Without turning his eyes away from the marching animals, the old man said, "Yes?"

"She's in there, right? I mean, we're gonna get her back."

"I don't know, Ella," he replied. "We can only do our best."

The front line broke its trot and started to run. The ground shook. An elephant knocked over a tree that was in his way. A rhino flattened a mailbox like a tin can.

Their footfalls reverberated like a long rip of thunder, startling birds into the sky.

The powerful animals dropped their heads and prepared to ram the wall.

"This is it," Ella said.

"I can't watch!" Richie announced. He pulled his cap over his eyes.

Noah placed his foot on the edge of the hippo's open mouth as if it were a step and climbed up to join Mr. Darby. He snatched the megaphone and hollered, "Go, Blizzard!"

Hearing Noah's voice, Blizzard jumped to the front of the pack. Just before he hit the wall, he turned his body to protect his head, struck the bricks, and plowed straight through. The other animals smashed forward in succession, and what was left of the wall exploded. Bricks shot in every direction, bouncing off buildings and shattering windows. Dust clouded the air as if a bomb had blasted.

Mr. Darby took back the megaphone and commanded, "Everybody—MOVE!"

The other animals charged forward: monkeys beside horses, giraffes beside cheetahs, crocodiles beside tigers. Thousands of animals barreled down the street.

Mr. Darby turned to the scouts and said, "Well? Are you ready to show us why you're called the Action Scouts?"

Ella reached over and lifted Richie's hat off his face.

"You're probably gonna want to see where you're going."

"What?" Richie asked. His eyes shifted nervously. "What happened?"

Noah jumped off the hippo and took off running to join the stampede. Ella ran after him, pumping her fist in the air. Richie followed, his reluctance evident in his skittish gait.

The scouts reached the rushing animals and found themselves in the middle of hundreds of white rabbits. Squinting in a cloud of dust, they charged through the open wall, straight into the unknown dangers of the Dark Lands.

CHAPTER 46

THE DARK LANDS

The scouts jumped aside to make room for the spectacular herds behind them. Noah looked around. The world ahead was draped in darkness. Shadows covered a gloomy forested landscape, blotted by a web of inky rivers and murky ponds. Stark mountains rose in the distance. Half-dead trees jutted from the dirt like the claws of buried monsters. Cords of lightning leaped between storm clouds and stabbed at the ground. Clouds hung heavily, as if they might crash from the sky. The animals pushed across the wet terrain, splashing water and mud.

"Well," Ella said, "they don't call this the Dark Lands

for nothing." She had intended to make a joke, but her voice quivered before she finished her sentence.

Behind her, a voice boomed, "It ain't a lack of light that gives this place its name. It's a lack of goodness."

The scouts spun around. Standing there was Tank, looking as big and bald as ever. His muscular body was as bumpy as the mountainsides.

"Tank!" Noah said. "You're gonna help?"

"Kid, I've been waiting to help with this operation for a long time."

Noah smiled. He turned and watched the last of the animals charge through the fallen wall. Crocodiles and seals dived into the rivers, and birds and bats filled the stormy sky. Monkeys, possums, and flying squirrels leaped through the trees.

The scouts were joined by their animal friends— Blizzard, Podgy, Dodie, and Little Bighorn. Marlo perched on Noah's shoulder. P-Dog and a dozen other prairie dogs scampered around Richie's feet.

"You guys ready?" Ella asked.

The animals grunted, snorted, chattered, and shuffled back and forth.

Noah climbed on Blizzard's back and said, "Let's find Megan!"

Ella ran to Little Bighorn and said, "Mind giving me a lift?" The rhino threw his head around and snorted his approval. Ella quickly climbed up and took her seat.

The troop headed into the Dark Lands. Dodie and Marlo flew up to search the treetops, while the prairie dogs raced in circles around everyone's feet, checking nooks and crannies in the ground.

"I don't see anything that looks like a sasquatch," Richie said to Tank. "Are they dead?"

"Maybe." Tank scanned the mountainsides and the forest. "Or maybe they're hiding."

In front of them, a pod of seals squirted out of the water and rushed clumsily along the shoreline, clapping their flippers against the muddy ground and chanting, *"Arrt! Arrt! Arrt!"*

The animals spread out as they journeyed deeper into the Dark Lands. Before long, the sounds of the city inhabitants faded, and the scouts found themselves alone with their group. The quiet was unnatural. It made Noah nervous.

"Guys," Ella said, "look at the hillside."

Noah looked up. He had trouble seeing the details until a flash of lightning lit the terrain. The hillside was covered with caves and crevices—all sorts of hiding places.

"Did anyone see that?" Richie moaned.

"Why do I suddenly feel like we're being watched?" Noah whispered.

"Stay up," Tank said. "Be prepared for anything.

Remember, nobody's been here for eighty years. Anything's possible."

Noah whistled for Marlo. The bird plunged from the sky and perched on his shoulder.

"Marlo, I need you to check those caves for sasquatches. Can you do that?"

Marlo chirped, sprang off Noah's shoulder, and flew toward the mountainside.

Tank walked to a pond and squatted. "Hmm."

"What is it, Tank?" Noah said.

"I don't know. It's too quiet. Something's making me nervous. This ain't making sense." Tank plucked a flashlight from his tool belt and shone it on a large footprint in the mud. "See that print?" He pointed the light at the distant ground, exposing more footprints. "All those prints are new. There—look at the mud. It's still wet."

"Maybe our animals did that."

"Nunh-unh," Tank said. "Only one animal leaves a print like that: a sasquatch. I've seen their prints a hundred times in our library books."

Spasms of lightning flashed over the landscape. Thunder boomed and echoed across the sky.

"They're here then," Noah said. "They're alive."

"This is *sooo* not good," Richie said. He bobbed his head nervously, causing the pom-pom on his cap to quiver. The prairie dogs zipped around his feet.

Marlo swooped down from the sky and landed on Noah's shoulder, chirping wildly. His beady black eyes almost popped out of his feathery face as he cocked his head from side to side.

"He's seen something," Tank said.

"A sasquatch?" Richie asked.

"I don't know. Maybe."

"Tank," Noah said, "let me use your flashlight."

Tank handed the flashlight to Noah, who shone it on the hillside. In an instant, his heart leaped into his throat. As he moved the beam from cave to cave, little points of light flashed back. Clusters glimmered in every cave—glowing spots of yellow bobbing in the darkness. What they were was obvious—eyes! The eyes of animals! And these animals' eyes were watching them.

Blizzard slunk forward and let out a slow, angry growl. Still on his back, Noah felt the bear's big muscles clenching.

"Sasquatches!" Tank said, and for the first time, Noah heard fear in the powerful man's voice—deep fear.

A bolt of lightning exposed a lone sasquatch racing down the mountainside. Noah struggled to focus his flashlight and saw a second beast charge behind the first. Another massive lightning bolt cracked the sky. Thunder boomed. Then dozens of sasquatches rocketed out of their caves, all raging toward the scouts.

In the Secret Zoo, the land of impossible things, a strange hillside was raining sasquatches—creatures that didn't exist, monstrous beasts trapped between animal and humankind. And in the Secret Zoo, the land of impossible things, a huge polar bear carrying a boy named Noah—a boy far from home, far from family, and far from the life he knew—charged forward, prepared for battle.

↪ CHAPTER 47 ↩

THE SASQUATCHES STRIKE

Blizzard barreled through the trees, flattening the underbrush beneath his mighty paws. Noah clung to the polar bear's neck, leaning so far forward that his chin repeatedly slammed down on Blizzard's head, leaving the taste of dirty fur in his mouth. The wind rushed across his cheeks and blew the flaps of his red hunting cap against his ears. Blizzard splashed through a river as if it were a puddle and blazed forward.

As the bear bore down on the first sasquatch, Noah had his first good look at the creature. Standing upright with its arms hanging down to its knees, indeed it was half ape and half human. Clumps of hair drooped from its elbows, knees, and toes like the matted fringes of an old stage curtain. At the sight of Blizzard, the sasquatch hunched over and raised its claws.

Blizzard planted his paws in the mud and sprayed it everywhere. Standing face-to-face, the two animals began to sidestep slowly in a circle, the way Noah had seen animals square off on TV. The sasquatch snarled, exposing thick square teeth and two pairs of fangs. Its yellow eyes and black pupils narrowed in on Blizzard.

Blizzard lowered his rear end to let Noah off. Noah backpedaled all the way to the edge of a nearby pond, which was as far away as he could go.

"Careful, Blizzard!" he called.

Blizzard and the sasquatch slunk from side to side. Blizzard let out a deep, slow growl. The sasquatch snorted and beat its fists against its chest. Each animal was studying its adversary. Then, in an instant, they jumped at each other and tumbled in a whirl of grunting, grabbing, and biting. Blizzard sank his teeth into the sasquatch's leg, and the sasquatch ripped a chunk of fur off the bear's back. They knocked each other into the trees and crushed the scrubby underbrush.

In horror, Noah watched, helpless. Then something seized his ankle. He glanced down and saw a sasquatch in the water, clutching his ankle. The beast had swum up silently behind him.

A flash of lightning revealed the creature's yellow eyes. Its long hair floated on the murky water like seaweed. It yanked Noah into the mud, knocking the wind out of him. Then it dragged the boy into the water. Noah tried to grab something, but his fingers found only mud and slid through it, leaving behind ten little trenches. He glanced up. The other sasquatch had its arms wrapped around Blizzard's head and was wrestling him to the ground. Blizzard was losing the fight, but that wasn't the worst of it. A gang of sasquatches was rushing in behind the mighty bear to finish him off.

Noah tried to scream but barely managed to wheeze. The sasquatch wrapped its claws around his other ankle and hauled him deeper into the pond. As Noah gasped for air, dirty pond water gushed over his head, and he swallowed that instead.

The sasquatch pulled him in deeper. And deeper. And deeper still. The farther Noah sank, the darker and colder the world grew. His heart pounded with fear. For the first time since Megan's disappearance, he doubted that he would see his sister again.

CHAPTER 48

THE BRAWL CONTINUES

Little Bighorn advanced through the trees, carrying Ella on his back, with Tank and Richie right behind. Suddenly Ella heard the clashing and grunting sounds of a fight. She looked ahead and spotted Blizzard squaring off with the sasquatch. With his head locked in the grip of the beast, he was being pulled down on his front legs and was struggling to keep his backside in the air.

Then she saw Noah—and that scared her senseless. A sasquatch was dragging him into a pond, and Noah was clawing desperately at the mud. Ella leaped off Little Bighorn and ran to the edge of the water, but by the time she got there, it was too late. Noah was gone! She dropped to her knees and stared across the water. Lightning flashed, revealing a few ripples, but nothing more.

"Richie!" she called out as she looked over her shoulder. "Did you see that?"

Richie had stopped ten feet from the water. His eyes wide with terror, he nodded his head.

Ella yelled for Podgy, but the penguin didn't need to be told what to do. He'd already swung into action, dashing toward the swampy water, the flat tops of his webbed feet flinging mud in all directions. Reaching the shore, he pushed off the edge and dived in.

Ella looked at Blizzard. The sasquatch had wrapped its arms around him and was bringing the bear down one leg at a time. Then she heard the thrashing of bushes and branches, and a gang of sasquatches charged out of the darkness. They piled on top of the great bear and drove him down to the muddy earth.

Tank and Little Bighorn stormed toward the sasquatches. The rhino dropped his head and pointed his horn straight ahead. To Ella, that horn was suddenly the deadliest weapon in the world.

Little Bighorn crashed into one sasquatch, but his horn just missed its stomach and passed harmlessly between its legs instead. With a quick snap of his neck, he flung the beast high in the air. Then he plowed into three other sasquatches, knocking them flat. Tank attacked the four sasquatches that had pinned down Blizzard. One by one, he seized them by the shoulders and hurled them off their feet.

"Excuse me!" Tank bellowed, "but you're sitting on my friend!"

Blizzard rolled to his feet and shook the confusion out of his head. He hurled his massive body forward and smashed into two sasquatches, bashing them down.

Ella's eyes darted to Richie. Prairie dogs were scampering around his feet, and some still stared at his heels. Even in this chaos, these critters wanted nothing more than Richie's long-gone sparkling shoes.

Ella threw up her arms and shouted, "Are you furballs gonna help or what?"

The prairie dogs glanced at one another with their noses and cheeks twitching, as if to say, "Is she talking to us?"

The next moment, a sasquatch that had just been flattened by one of Tank's crushing right hooks slithered through the mud, right up to the prairie dogs. It lay in front of them, stunned. P-Dog jumped, landed on the creature's head, and bit the tip of its flat, upturned nose. The sasquatch emitted an ugly guttural wail and rolled over in the mud, clutching its snout. Taking their cue from P-Dog, the prairie dogs charged the other beasts.

They bit their heels and long-haired toes.

Marlo and Dodie assailed the enemy from above. They swooped down and jabbed the sasquatches with their pointed beaks.

"Ella!" Richie said.

Ella turned. Richie now stood at the edge of the pond, gazing across the dark water.

"I don't see Noah!" he said. "I can't see a trace of him!"

"How long have they been down there?"

"Too long!"

"Should we go in after him?" Ella asked.

Richie looked back and forth between Ella and the pond, but he couldn't speak.

"Richie! Should we go in after him?"

"I—I don't know!" he stammered. "I think our only hope is Podgy!"

They had nothing else to say. They could only wait.

Ella turned back to the brawl and saw Tank head-butt a sasquatch and toss the beast aside. Little Bighorn and Blizzard were grappling with a mob of sasquatches. The huge animals stomped on bushes and snapped trees in two. The prairie dogs were still scrambling in the mix, chomping on the heels and hairy toes of the sasquatches.

Richie grabbed Ella's shoulder and said, "This is madness!"

The Dark Lands were in chaos. Countless sasquatches

werc storming down the mountainside and racing for the opening in the wall. Some of the animals from the Secret Society were trying to fight them back, but most were losing. All around, they lay in the mud, unconscious or worse. On top of this, there was no sign of Megan. The world was falling apart.

"We've been set up," Ella said flatly.

"What?"

"This whole thing. The sasquatches have been holding Megan prisoner knowing we'd eventually crash through that wall and come after her. This is their first chance in eighty years to escape."

Ella's eyes widened as she watched a sasquatch kick P-Dog. The prairie dog flew through the air and splashed down in the pond. He tried to paddle with his minuscule front legs but sank almost instantly.

"P-Dog!" Richie cried out.

Richie started toward the pond, but Ella seized his elbow. "Wait!" She pointed into the sky. "Look up!"

The scouts tilted back their heads just in time to see Dodie dive straight at the pond. If he wasn't being heroic, he would have looked comical with his wimpy wings pumping and his oversized beak weighing down his face. The dodo hit the pond and splashed water in every direction. A moment later, he emerged and rose into the air clutching the prairie dog by his rear end. P-Dog's eyes darted around as he tried to pinpoint what had gone wrong in the last ten seconds of his life. Dodie circled in the air and dropped him into Richie's open arms.

"Are you all right?" Richie asked.

P-Dog just blinked and buried himself in the cradle of Richie's arms, looking like a fat furry baby.

"Richie," Ella said, "how long has it been now? For Noah, I mean."

Richie didn't answer, and his silence was frightening.

Ella leaned toward the lake and whispered, "C'mon, Noah! C'mon, Podgy!"

Around them, the battle raged. The sasquatches were winning.

CHAPTER 49

PODGY TO THE RESCUE

The sasquatch pulled Noah into the depths of the water. Noah kicked and pulled, but it didn't help. With such an insignificant amount of light, he could barely see. Seaweed tangled around his arms and legs and stroked his neck with its slime. He needed air more than he'd ever needed anything in his life. He was dizzy and nauseated, and his heart was pounding.

The sasquatch was staring at him. Noah could see that its eyes were open and gleaming, only inches from his face. The beast was enjoying watching Noah struggle for his life. For the sasquatch, this was fun.

As Noah prepared for the worst, he caught a faint view of something swimming above. It looked like a silhouette moving against deeper shadows. As it neared, Noah made out its oval body and long flippers. It was Podgy!

Podgy circled the sasquatch's head. He circled twice, three times. The beast's eyes followed the rotation, confused. Noah made out a thick cord of seaweed in Podgy's bill. As the penguin swam, he looped the seaweed around the beast's neck. The fourth time, he tightened the cord. The sasquatch let go of Noah and swiped at Podgy, missing him completely. In the darkness, the animals struggled, bumping into Noah and thrashing him about.

Podgy chomped down on both ends of the seaweed and swam up the way he'd come, tightening the weed like a noose. The weight of the sasquatch stalled the penguin, and Podgy found himself treading water, pumping his flippers but going nowhere. Choking, the sasquatch reached to free its throat. Podgy dropped the seaweed, darted between the sasquatch's legs, snagged Noah by his shirt collar, and bolted to the surface. They squirted out of the pond and slid onto the muddy shore.

Ella and Richie spotted their friends and rushed to their aid.

"Noah!" Ella cried out. "Are you okay?"

Noah coughed and spit up water uncontrollably.

Within seconds, the sasquatch appeared near the middle

of the pond and headed for shore. It swam through the deep water until it could stand. Then it broke into a run with its arms waving and its claws extended. Ella screamed.

The scouts heard pounding footsteps and looked through the trees. Little Bighorn was charging with his spike lowered. The children dived to the side, and the rhino blasted past, nearly squashing Noah. When the sasquatch saw Little Bighorn, its wicked snarl went limp. An instant later, the rhino's spike speared the beast. The sasquatch flew backward and splashed into the water. Dead, the beast floated on its stomach with its long-haired arms spread out at its sides. Repulsed, Noah looked away.

Ella crawled to Noah. "Are you okay?"

Noah nodded, but he continued to cough up water.

"Listen!" Richie said. He jumped up and stared into the distance. "I hear Mr. Darby."

Over the battle sounds, the scouts heard Mr. Darby's voice, distant but clear. He was ordering everyone to fall back to the city, because sasquatches were escaping from their sector.

"No!" Ella said, shaking her head in disbelief. "This is our fault!"

Blizzard and the prairie dogs joined the scouts. They'd won their battle. The sasquatches that weren't dead or unconscious were running away.

Gasping for breath, Tank said, "We gotta get outta here! There are too many of them! No one expected this!"

Noah managed to stand up. Panting, he wiped his mouth and said, "Go . . . without me. I'll . . . catch up."

"Noah, no!" Ella yelled. "You heard Mr. Darby! There's no chance—"

Noah leaned his palms against his knees and struggled to pull more air into his lungs. Then he said, "Tell Mr. Darby to drop the boulders. I'll make my way out somehow, but not without Megan."

Tank was about to say something, but Ella cut in. "Noah, please! I can't lose another friend!"

"You won't," Noah said. "You'll be getting back the one you lost."

Ella was quiet. Noah saw that she finally understood that he intended to leave this place with Megan . . . or not at all. He stepped forward and took the hands of his two friends.

"Go," he said. "I promise, when this is all done, we'll be eating lunch together in Fort Scout—all four of us."

The scouts hugged. For a moment, Noah forgot where he was. He forgot the danger, the fear, and the pain. All that existed was the love he shared with his best friends.

"Come back with Megan," Ella said.

"I will," Noah promised. He faced their brawny friend

and said, "Tank, you gotta get these guys outta here."

Tank held Noah's gaze. Then the massive man gave him a quick nod and switched his attention to the others. "Let's go, gang!"

Everyone but Blizzard turned and ran. Blizzard padded toward Noah, but Noah held up his hand to stop him.

"Go, Blizzard. My friends need you."

Blizzard hesitated; he blinked a few times. Then he turned and headed after the others. Noah stood and watched them all go, treasuring the image of his friends. He couldn't help wondering if this was the last time he'd see them.

When they disappeared into the foggy night, Noah shifted his thoughts. He sloshed through the mud and advanced deeper into the Dark Lands.

Alone.

༄ CHAPTER 50 ༄

THE FLAG

Lightning cracked. Thunder boomed. A chilly wind blew down from the hillside. Noah marched on.

All around him, animals from the Secret Zoo were rushing toward the exit of the sector, trying to get out quickly so Mr. Darby could seal the wall again. Time and again, Noah caught sight of sasquatches. Each time, he ducked into the underbrush and lay in silence until they passed.

"How did all this happen?" Noah grumbled.

He neared the hillside and the caves, and he contemplated how many sasquatches might be there. He wondered if they were waiting for him.

"What the—!"

Something cold and flat had stroked his leg. He jolted sideways and clunked his head on a tree branch. When he collected himself and looked down, he saw none other than Podgy. As usual, the penguin looked casual, cool, and unconcerned.

Noah whispered, "I thought you were with everyone else. What happened?"

Podgy waddled up to Noah and flapped his flippers. Clearly he wasn't going to leave Noah alone in this dreadful land.

"You shouldn't have come back," Noah said. He considered this for a moment and then added, "But I'm glad you did."

Together the boy and the penguin headed for the hillside, keeping a watchful eye on the sasquatches as they raced toward the City of Species. One minute, the beasts lurched forward like apes on their four limbs, and the next, they ran like humans on their back legs. The creatures seemed confused about their bodies, as if they weren't sure how they worked best.

Noah and Podgy neared the mountainside, and each time the electric sky pulsed, Noah discerned more details of the terrain. When they started to climb, he thought he saw a scrap of color in front of one of the caves. He stopped walking and peered at the spot. Nothing. He hoped the light wasn't playing tricks on his eyes in this desolate land, and he caught up with Podgy. As they ascended along a rough path, sheer rock rose to their left.

Five minutes later, Noah whispered, "Podgy! Look!"

Fifty feet above them, at the edge of a rock wall, was the dark entrance to the cave that had grabbed Noah's attention. Wedged in the rock was a stick with a red flag tied to the end.

"It's Megan."

❧ CHAPTER 51 ❧

PODGY TAKES OFF

"Podgy," he said, "we've got to get up to that cave. Megan's in there! I'm sure of it."

The flag was waving back and forth. Noah squinted, but he couldn't make out any details in the darkness. Podgy stared at his friend with a blank expression. The boy leaned forward and grabbed the penguin's flippers.

"Podge," he said, "I need you to get us up there. I need you . . . to fly!"

Podgy flinched as if he couldn't believe what Noah was saying.

"You can do it, Podge! I saw your buddy out on the ice.

He flew! And I know you can, too. You just have to want to! You just have to believe you can do it!"

Podgy backed away.

"It's not that high! What? Fifty feet, maybe."

Podgy stared up at the cave and back at Noah.

"C'mon! You gotta try! Megan's up there, and time is running out. Climbing would take forever!"

Podgy glanced from the cave to Noah and back again.

"We've already practiced this. In the water, remember? I rode on your back, and it was easy! How is this different, huh? You just flap your flippers, right?"

Podgy took a step toward the cave. The light in his black eyes sparkled.

"We'll do it like this. You take off running, and I'll follow you. When you start to go up, I'll jump on your back, and . . . *whooooosh*!" Noah swept his hands up in the air.

Podgy thought about it. A moment later, he took off running, waddling back and forth as fast as he could.

Noah chased him. "All right, Podge!"

The big penguin leaned forward and picked up speed. His flat feet slapped the mud. He stuck out his flippers and flapped them up and down.

"Go, Podgy!" Noah screamed.

Rabbits, monkeys, and squirrels were still passing them on their way to the safety of the city. Above them, electric clouds spit out lightning and thunder. Noah and Podgy remained focused on their task: getting sky beneath the wings of a penguin!

Podgy's strides grew longer and fuller. Then . . . he jumped! The instant he left the ground, Noah wrapped his arms around him. The penguin dipped . . . and bobbed . . . and he climbed into the air. Two feet, three feet, four feet—up, up, up!

Then he began to wobble like a small airplane in a turbulent sky.

"Keep steady!" Noah hollered.

His advice didn't help. When Podgy reached seven feet above the ground, he lost control, veered to the side, and crashed—straight into a gang of sasquatches! The beasts tumbled like giant bowling pins. Everyone slammed to the ground and started to roll down the mountain. When they came to a stop, they were covered in mud.

Noah and Podgy untangled themselves and jumped to their feet. So did their enemies. For a moment, the creatures stood on their four limbs like apes. Then they charged, heaving their weight back and forth and sloshing their knuckles in the mud.

Podgy and Noah took off through the trees. The sasquatches chased them, grunting, panting, and kicking mud everywhere. Other gangs realized what was happening. From every direction on the mountainside, they ran toward Noah and Podgy. This time, Podgy had no choice. He flapped his flippers, preparing to fly.

"We gotta do this!" Noah yelled.

As the sasquatches closed in on them, Podgy's strides grew longer and stronger. The beasts were so close that Noah could smell them. They had a putrid odor—a cross between muck and sewage.

"Go!" Noah screamed. His voice quivered with fear. *"Nooowww!"*

Podgy jumped into his strides and rose into the air. Noah leaped on his back, clung to his neck, and felt his shoes leave the ground.

Podgy went up . . . up . . . and up! Six feet, seven feet, eight feet! Noah looked down and saw the sasquatches' long arms swiping at his heels.

"Yes!" Noah yelled. "Keep going!"

All at once, the sasquatches crashed into one another. They stumbled and fell like cartoon characters. Noah saw the soles of their feet as they rolled. He cupped one hand to his mouth and cried, "You're gonna have to grow wings if you wanna catch the Action Scouts!"

Podgy sailed into the stormy sky. Once he was above the trees, he skirted the top branches as if he'd been flying his whole life. Then he flew higher. Noah guessed that they were sixty feet off the ground. From this height, he had a good view of everything in the Dark Lands.

"The cave!" Noah said. "Right there! Do you see it?"

Podgy dipped down and headed toward the mountain. He skimmed the treetops so closely that Noah felt the twigs skip off his toes. As Podgy flew toward the cave, Noah peered inside, but it was too dark to see anything.

"Careful, Podge!" Noah warned.

Podgy straightened out, aimed for the entrance, and prepared to touch down. Though a natural in the air, he was a tyro at landing. The penguin slammed to the ground. He and Noah swallowed dirt and dust as they reeled and tumbled into the cave. Eventually they rolled to a stop.

The cave was pitch black. Noah couldn't see Podgy. The only light came from the dim, stormy sky outside the entrance. He peered out and was able to discern the dark silhouette of the flag.

"Megan!" Noah screamed. He jumped to his feet and ran forward. "Megan! I can't believe we finally—"

Near the entrance, someone ripped the flag off the stick and stepped into the light. Noah slid to a halt and stared. It wasn't his sister. It was a sasquatch—the most monstrous beast he'd seen yet.

CHAPTER 52

THE CAVE

The sasquatch crept forward. Its long, knotted tufts of hair swung from its arms and knees, and its apelike grunts rumbled inside the walls of the cave. As Noah's eyes adjusted to the new darkness, he could make out the creature's claws. Long and swollen, they looked infected. Noah backpedaled, searching for any idea of what to do next. The only way out seemed to be the way they'd come in.

Something jabbed at his back. He shrieked, certain that it was the claw of another sasquatch, and spun around. There was Podgy; Noah had stepped into his bill.

Together Podgy and Noah retreated farther into the cave to keep space between the sasquatch and themselves.

Noah focused on the flag in the sasquatch's hand with the letters *A* and *S*. There was no doubt—it was Megan's distress flag.

A soft voice came from the back of the cave: "Noah? Noah, is that you?"

Someone was standing in the shadows.

"Megan?"

"It's me!"

They ran into each other's arms. Noah went limp with relief, and for a second, he worried that he might collapse. He pulled his head back for a look at his sister and fought to raise her image from the darkness. She looked thin and tired. She'd managed to keep her glasses, and her pigtails—still in place—were matted and dirty.

"I saw it all," Megan said. "I saw the wall explode. I saw the animals charge in. And somehow I knew it was you. I had my flag and I used it, but that awful thing saw me. It took my flag and lured you in here—you and . . ." Megan glanced at Podgy and changed her thought. "Was that penguin just flying?"

"Yeah."

"When did he learn to do that?"

"About two minutes ago, I guess."

"What?"

"Never mind that now. We gotta get outta here."

Swaying back and forth, the sasquatch moved closer. It was hunched over to keep its head from dragging along the ceiling of the cave. The ugly beast dropped the flag and stepped on it.

"What now, Podgy?" Noah asked.

Podgy glanced at his friend, nodded his head, and suddenly charged forward—directly at the sasquatch. When he reached the creature, he ducked and darted through its legs. The beast swiped at Podgy, lost its balance, and nearly toppled over. Podgy whirled around and dashed back between its hairy limbs. The sasquatch lashed out once more and just missed the elusive penguin. In disgust, it rolled back its head and let out an apelike roar that boomed and echoed against the walls of the cave.

"Is your friend *trying* to get us killed?" Megan asked.

Noah paused for a moment. Then he said, "He's trying to save us."

"What? How?"

"He's distracting him. Knocking him off-balance."

"For what?"

Noah turned to Megan and smiled. "Wanna go for a ride on a penguin?"

"Excuse me?"

"I think he wants to carry us out of here—both at the same time."

"Can he do that?"

"We'll find out."

Podgy waddled back toward Noah and Megan, ran a full circle around them, and charged the sasquatch again.

"He's ready," Noah said. "Are you?"

"No!" Fear rippled her voice. "Not at all."

Noah gave his sister a peck on the cheek. "I never thought I'd say this, but I've missed you."

He turned around, faced the sasquatch, and took a deep breath. A second later, he charged, screaming, *"Rrraaahhh!"*

Megan raced behind him, shrieking and pumping her arms at her sides.

Stunned, the sasquatch stepped back. Then, as if it remembered how big and ominous it was, the beast stepped forward, raised its meaty hands, and showed its dreadful claws. Podgy ducked again, posturing to shoot between its legs. Seeing this, the sasquatch leaned down to grab him, but this time, the penguin pounced on its head and hopped over it. The sasquatch spun around to grab the bird, but missed again. Podgy had distracted the creature long enough for Megan and Noah to escape through its legs and head for the opening of the cave.

"Run, Podgy!" Noah screamed.

Podgy was already racing for the exit faster than Noah had ever seen him move. The sasquatch dropped onto its knuckles like an ape and chased him. At the mouth of the cave, the scouts braced themselves.

"I don't think this is gonna work!" Megan shrieked.

"There's no time to think!" Noah shouted.

A moment later, Podgy blasted out of the cave into the stormy sky. Noah leaped onto his back and grabbed his neck. When he expected to feel Megan land behind him, he instead felt nothing. He looked over his shoulder. The wretched sasquatch had clasped Megan by the ankle and was dangling her over the cliff. The beast had nabbed her in mid-jump.

"Podgy!" Noah yelled. "That thing's got my sister!"

Podgy flew in a wide arc and navigated along the mountainside. As he passed the cave, he whacked the sasquatch's head with his flipper. The sasquatch floundered on the cliff, flailing its arms. Then it lost its grip on Megan's ankle, and both of them fell over the edge, plummeting toward the murky ground below.

Podgy dived so suddenly that Noah nearly toppled off his back. The penguin swooped beside Megan, and at just the right moment, Noah reached out and snagged his sister by the wrist.

The dive-and-catch was a spectacular feat, but Megan's additional weight was too much for Podgy to bear. The penguin lost control and crashed into the top of a tall, full tree. The threesome fell through the branches,

THE CAVE 279

bouncing off the large ones and crashing through the thin ones, until they landed with a series of thuds at the base of the trunk. Twigs and leaves showered down on them.

"Everyone okay?" Megan asked.

"Yeah," Noah said. "Podgy, you okay?"

Podgy stood up and shook his body the way a wet dog does.

Noah looked around. He realized that they must have been a sensational sight in the air, because sasquatches were approaching from every direction, dodging trees and leaping over bushes. Within seconds, the scouts were surrounded by a small gang of them. They were grunting, snorting, and looking anxious to rip limbs from bodies. A lightning bolt split the sky, and the yellow of their eyes glowed.

The beasts scrambled to clear a pathway for a single sasquatch to come forward. The newcomer walked with a limp and had a swollen bald patch on the side of its head. It looked as if it had just been smacked with a large stick—or maybe something of equal size and shape, like a penguin's flipper.

"Not good," Noah said.

The scouts and Podgy backed against the tree.

"Sorry, Megan," Noah said. "I thought—I thought I could get you out of here."

Megan scanned the dark landscape for an escape. "It's not over yet," she said.

"There's no way out," Noah said. "Not unless you come up with a miracle."

"I think it's coming our way."

Their miracle was charging toward them from behind the sasquatches. Storming through the muddy forest were Ella, Richie, Tank, Blizzard, Little Bighorn, Dodie, Marlo, P-Dog, and a bunch of other prairie dogs. Ella was riding on Little Bighorn, and Richie was on Blizzard. They plowed into the sasquatches and sent them flying. Some landed in the trees unconscious, draped over the branches like laundry that was hung out to dry. Panic-stricken, the remaining creatures scattered. Blizzard growled. Little Bighorn snorted. The prairie dogs yipped like mad.

"Guys!" Noah shouted. "What are you doing back here?"

Tank said, "Marlo spotted Podgy soaring through the air like a little blimp. We knew something was up when you flew into that cave."

Megan ran to greet Ella and Richie, shouting, "I didn't know if I'd ever see you—"

Tank scooped Megan up and slung her on top of Little Bighorn behind Ella.

"Maybe we should save the hugs and kisses for later," he boomed. "What do you say?"

"Good idea," Ella said. She swatted the rhino's side and called, "C'mon, Little Bighorn! Let's ride!"

Noah turned to Tank. "Thanks for—"

Before he could finish, Tank lifted him by his pants and tossed him on top of Blizzard.

"No time for chitchat, kid. Any second now, Mr. Darby's gonna close up shop, if you know what I'm saying. I asked him to keep the wall down for ten more minutes."

"Ten minutes?" Noah said.

"Less than that now."

Noah adjusted himself behind Richie and said, "You heard him, Bliz! Let's get outta here!"

As Blizzard raced off, Noah glanced over his shoulder. The prairie dogs were scurrying behind them as fast as their short legs could run. In the sky, Dodie and Marlo were joined by Podgy, their newfangled flying friend. Tank was on his way to the exit when a sasquatch—a huge one with a chunk of hair missing from the side of its swollen face—grabbed him from behind. Tank swung around and knocked it out with a single punch.

"Sometimes," Noah muttered, "things end on a high note."

The motley herd of animals raced across the Dark Lands, back to the City of Species. Noah thought of bringing Megan home, and a hundred emotions washed over him. He was so overcome by love, joy, and relief that he started to cheer and wave his arms. The other scouts looked at him with big smiles. They, too, yelled and pumped their fists. That moment assured them that nothing would ever divide their friendship—no enchanted lands, no beastly creatures, and not even time. Real friendship was stronger than anything else in the world.

They charged ahead and reached the exit. The instant they barreled through, the elephants dropped the boulders. The moment the boulders slammed the street, a troop of monkeys sprang into action, sliding the velvet curtains down from the branches to seal off the Dark Lands.

Once again, the City of Species was safe under the magic that had issued from the fingertips of three mystical brothers from a distant land.

✦ CHAPTER 53 ✦

GOOD-BYE

The scouts stood beside the curtain to Sector 15, ready to go home, a place Megan had not been for three long weeks. Mr. Darby, Tank, and the scouts' animal friends stood beside them.

Tank said, "About Megan . . ."

The scouts waited for more. When nothing came, Noah said, "Yeah?"

"I met with a few of the Descenders. We came up with a plan about—"

"The *who*?" Ella asked.

Tank shook off the question. "Never mind who they are

for now. Just know that I talked to them, and we have an idea to hide the reason Megan disappeared. We thought of something to tell your parents—your *world*—about Megan, about what happened to her. It would keep the secrets of the zoo safe."

Noah was genuinely curious. "Let's hear it."

Tank started talking, and for the next ten minutes, the scouts listened and nodded and asked questions. After hearing the plan, they agreed to try it. Noah thought it was a great idea; he just didn't know if they could pull it off.

Finally Noah turned to Mr. Darby and asked, "What about the sasquatches? How many got out?"

"It's difficult to say. We posted koalas in the trees. They spotted around fifty."

"What will they do?" Megan asked. "The sasquatches, I mean."

"Perhaps nothing," Mr. Darby said. "But I fear that I'm thinking wishfully."

"I feel terrible," Richie said. "It's like—"

"Please don't! You rescued your friend. This was your duty. What's more, in rescuing Megan, I believe you rescued us."

"Rescued you?" Ella said. "How?"

"The Megan Situation is over, and the division it created in the Secret Society will no longer exist. We'll be united again. We need unity to focus on our task, which is protecting the Secret Zoo—its animals and its magic."

"I wish we could help," Noah said.

Mr. Darby raised one eyebrow. "Well, you can. We need Crossers—people that pass between the Outside and the Inside. We need good people. Adventurous people! Scouts would do nicely."

"Action Scouts," Tank said, and winked.

"Mr. Darby," Ella said, "we're—we're only kids!"

"Only kids!" Mr. Darby barked. He laughed and patted her head. "Only kids! Look at all you've done! The Action Scouts are much more than kids, I assure you."

Noah said, "I'm not sure if—"

Mr. Darby raised his palm. "Think about it. For now, go back to your homes and families."

"Before we leave, I'd like to say good-bye to my friends."

Noah ran to Blizzard, who waited behind Mr. Darby with solemn eyes and his ears pressed flat against his head. Noah wrapped his arms around him. "Good-bye, Bliz," he said. "I'll miss you."

Ella and Richie ran to either side of Blizzard and squeezed the giant polar bear, burying their cheeks in his furry sides. Blizzard rolled his head back and roared. His voice echoed off the city walls, and the birds in the tree branches erupted into mournful chirruping and cawing.

The scouts said good-bye to Little Bighorn and Marlo and Dodie and Tank.

Richie bent down to the group of prairie dogs that lay at his feet, and P-Dog sprang up. Richie scratched him behind the ears and said, "Listen, if you guys find the gorilla that stole my shoes, do me a favor and drop them in the mail."

Petting Podgy's feathered head, Megan said, "Thanks for everything, little dude! Without you, I'd still be trapped in that cave."

Noah looked at Podgy. "I can hardly believe we did it!" he said as he leaned forward to hug the big penguin. Then Podgy did a remarkable thing—he wrapped his flippers around Noah and hugged him back.

"Whoa, boy! Easy with those flippers," Noah said. "Those are your ticket to the sky."

Podgy flapped his flippers and Noah noticed that, for the first time, the penguin didn't look sad and bored. Light gleamed in his eyes.

"It wasn't his flippers that got him flying," Mr. Darby said. "It was the strength of his spirit. That's a power you showed him."

Noah smiled and gazed affectionately at Podgy, who was still flapping his flippers. "Good-bye, Podge. I'll see you around, huh? At Penguin Palace in the Clarksville City Zoo . . . or . . ." Noah glanced at the animals and the trees and the streets of the City of Species. "Or elsewhere!"

As the scouts walked toward the doorway that led homeward, Mr. Darby called out, "You'll think about it, then? My proposition? A society as great as ours could use your help."

The children's eyes met briefly, and Noah replied, "Keep in touch, Mr. Darby. You know how."

"Indeed I do," the old man said with a grin. "Indeed I do."

The Action Scouts—complete again, with Megan back—waved good-bye to Mr. Darby, Tank, Blizzard, Podgy, Little Bighorn, and the other animals who had gathered to see them off: pandas, cheetahs, kangaroos, tigers, turtles, and countless others. They lined the streets, the buildings, and the trees.

Hot tears formed in Noah's eyes. The only thing that stopped them from falling was the awareness that he was leaving the magic and beauty of the Secret Zoo to take his sister to her rightful place in their family.

The scouts pushed through the velvet curtain and entered Sector 15. The curtain fell closed, leaving behind the City of Species with the animals and people the scouts had quickly grown to love.

CHAPTER 54

HELLO

As Noah and Megan rounded a long curve on Jenkins Street, their home came into view. Little more than fifty yards away, it sat on a slight hill. Two police cars were parked in the street in front of the house. A few people were out on their lawns and front porches, curious about the commotion at the Nowicki house.

"What time is it, Noah?" Megan asked.

He shrugged. "Nine o'clock, maybe."

Noah realized his entire adventure in the Secret Zoo had spanned less than nine hours. That amount seemed impossibly short, but then Noah realized how quickly everything had happened. Crossing Arctic Town, exploring the City of Species, escaping the heights of the Forest of Flight, talking to Mr. Darby in Hummingbird Hideout, rescuing Megan from the Dark Lands—every step of the way had taken less than an hour.

Their neighbor Mr. Peters was raking dead leaves off his front lawn. As they passed his house, Mr. Peters absently lifted his head and said, "Noah," without pausing in his labors. When he detected who was walking next to Noah, he started to say her name until surprise stopped him short: "Meg—"

Megan just smiled and waved.

The rake slipped from Mr. Peters's grasp and was swallowed by the pile of leaves. His body stiffened, his jaw dropped, and for a second he looked as witless as a zombie. When his senses came back, he turned and ran into his house, calling out his wife's name again and again, his voice echoing off the houses and causing a commotion.

As the two scouts headed up the street, their neighbors took notice of them from the windows of their homes. They poured onto their front lawns, kicking through leaves in slippers and bare feet. Some were silent, and others cheered. They clutched their hearts and covered their gaping mouths. Mrs. Sanders fell to her knees and began to pray. Megan was home, and it was a miracle.

Noah and Megan smiled at their neighbors as they

passed. To Noah, the moment was as surreal as anything he'd experienced in the Secret Zoo. Noah was bringing his missing sister home, and the streets were erupting with joy, relief, and love.

As they neared the house, their mother and father peeked out their front door at the scene, spotted their children, and charged out of the house. The scouts ran to them, and they met on the sidewalk. Megan and her mother rushed into each other's arms, and Megan's mother burst into tears. She pressed her face against her daughter's and stroked her hair. Noah watched as Megan, too, began to cry—softly, at first, but then more easily, until she was sobbing. Noah understood their emotions. He knew where they came from. They issued forth from a place too complicated and deep and beyond explanation to be called anything but "the heart."

As Noah's father dropped to his knees and partly wrapped himself in his son, tears poured from Noah's cheeks.

Noah's sister was alive. And she was home.

❧ AFTERWORD ❧
HIGH UP IN FORT SCOUT

Two weeks had passed since Megan's return. Carrying a plate of sandwiches, Noah walked across his backyard, climbed the ladder to Fort Scout, and joined his sister and friends high in the tree. He set the plate down, and each of them snatched a sandwich. Already life was getting back to normal.

They ate in silence. Richie picked up the binoculars, walked to the window, and scanned the zoo.

"See anyone we know?" Ella asked.

"Nope. Not yet," he said. "Wait a minute! Look at this guy." He passed Noah the binoculars.

Noah looked through the lenses and smiled. Blizzard

lay on a block of ice in Arctic Town. He had stretched out his legs, crossed his paws, and rested his chin on top of them, as if they were a pillow. He was watching a group of curious children not much younger than Megan.

Noah passed the binoculars around. The scouts shared a laugh as they recalled their own visits to the zoo before their secret journey. They spent the rest of the afternoon hanging out in the fort, telling jokes, giggling, and talking. They discussed many things, but the topic repeatedly returned to the Secret Zoo and the future of the Action Scouts.

Afternoon turned into evening, and Fort Scout received a visitor. This visitor didn't climb the ladder to enter from below. Tiny and blue feathered, he swooped from the treetops and landed on Noah's shoulder.

"Marlo!" the scouts called out together.

This was the first time they'd seen him since they left the City of Species. Marlo tipped his head from side to side and blinked hastily. In his beak was a folded slip of paper.

"Is that for us?" Noah asked.

The malachite kingfisher dropped the paper in his lap. Noah stared down at it, not knowing what to do.

"Any chance you'll be opening that before Christmas?" Ella asked. "If not, I'm gonna go home and get a warmer jacket."

Noah unfolded the paper and glanced at the signature.

"It's from Mr. Darby."

"And?"

"It's too dark. I can't see what's—"

Ella snatched a penlight from Richie's pocket—a new one, since he'd lost his other in Rhinorama—and handed it to Noah.

"Here! Now you can read it."

Noah switched on the light and shone it across the page. Marlo sidestepped toward Noah's neck and looked down, as if he were reading, too. Noah's eyes grew so big that they almost popped out of his face.

"What?" Megan questioned. "What does it say?"

Noah said nothing.

"C'mon," Richie said. "What is it?"

Noah cleared his throat and said, "Mr. Darby wants to know if—"

He was interrupted by the sound of his mother calling them indoors.

"Coming, Mom!" Megan shouted back. She climbed to her feet and dusted off her jeans. "Let's talk inside."

Noah looked at Marlo. "Can you come back tomorrow? Tell Mr. Darby I'll have an answer to his question by then."

Marlo chirped twice and shot back into the trees.

"What question?" Ella asked.

Noah gazed at his friends and his sister and said, "Guys, we have a lot to talk about."

Before he could finish, Mrs. Nowicki called a second time.

Noah said, "Mom's waiting. We'll talk inside."

Ella and Megan jumped on the slide and coasted to the ground. Richie climbed down the ladder, and Noah slid down the rope. Together the four children dashed across the lawn to the back porch. Running made them giddy. They laughed and shouted and waved their arms in the air. Playfully Ella bumped Richie into the hedge and Megan tripped Noah. They pushed their way inside and slammed the door on the night.

Little did they know what a good thing that was. Because not only had they slammed the door on the night, but they'd also shut out something else. Someone was outside—hiding, watching, and waiting in the shadows. The inhabitants of the Secret Zoo knew this man as the Shadowist, but only a few believed he still existed. Mr. Darby and Tank were among those few.

A hundred years ago, the Shadowist had gone by another name. The name was DeGraff. A hundred years ago, he'd stood on Mr. Jackson's rain-drenched porch. A hundred years ago, he'd told a tale about a magical man named Bhanu. A hundred years ago, Mr. DeGraff had been responsible for creating the Secret Zoo.

What will happen next to the Action Scouts?

Read on for a preview of

THE SECRET ZOO

SECRETS AND SHADOWS

❦ CHAPTER 8 ❦

A PROPOSITION AT THE FOUNTAIN FORUM

𝕿he scouts were silent. They sat perfectly still atop Blizzard and Little Bighorn. In the group around Mr. Darby, only the prairie dogs moved, continuously stirring up leaves as they dashed around the ankles of the polar bear and the rhino.

For Noah, Mr. Darby's words jarred a memory of the scouts' first meeting with Tank, outside of Creepy Critters. At that time, Tank alluded to someone being in danger, and when Richie asked who, Tank simply replied, "Everyone—the whole world." Now, two weeks later, Mr. Darby had insinuated the same thing.

Hannah finally ended the silence by popping a bubble

and letting the gum smack her mouth. She licked the thin, sticky paste from her lips.

"Ooo-kay," said Richie, his voice quivering. "All this talk from you guys about the world ending and stuff—it's really starting to freak me out."

"I'm with Richie," said Noah.

"Understandably," answered Mr. Darby. "It comes with the territory of our plight."

Ella said, "Let's hear this proposition—the one where we help save the world."

The old man whisked his book off his chair and plopped back into the cushions. He swept one side of his trench coat over his legs and flattened the wrinkles with his palm. Noah found it a bit odd that he would cover himself. Could he possibly be cold?

"Over the past two weeks, I've spoken at great length with the Secret Council, and we have unanimously decided to offer you the opportunity to become Crossers."

"Crossers . . ." said Noah. "You mentioned this the last time we were here. What exactly is a Crosser?"

Mr. Darby gathered his bushy beard in his hand and stroked it to a point. "A Crosser, in its simplest terms, is someone who passes between our zoos—the Clarksville Zoo and the Secret Zoo. A Crosser can *cross* from one zoo to the other, *cross* an entire sector, or *cross* from a sector into the City of Species."

"Like we just did," said Ella. "Through Metr-APE-olis."

"Exactly so." Mr. Darby stroked his beard again and continued. "As you know, the Clarksville Zoo exhibits have hidden entrances to different sectors of the Secret Zoo—sectors that connect to the City of Species, the core of our kingdom. Though these entrances were made for animals, our human Crossers use them, too. A Crosser's biggest responsibility is to guard these entrances, which we call sector gateways, or simply gateways. To do this successfully, Crossers are trained to effectively cross any sector."

"Are they all human?" Richie asked. "The Crossers, I mean."

"Not at all." Mr. Darby turned to Megan. "Remember the monkeys you spotted on the rooftops of your neighborhood when this all began?"

Megan recalled the incident clearly and nodded. "They weren't supposed to be there, right? They snuck out of the zoo?"

Mr. Darby couldn't restrain a smile. "Oh, they snuck out of the zoo, but they were definitely supposed to be there. They were Crossers—Crossers that patrol the border of the Clarksville Zoo. Some animals post in the trees of your neighborhood at night. We—"

"Whoa!" Ella said. "Did you just say you *they post in our trees*!"

Mr. Darby nodded. "Indeed."

"Since when?" Ella asked.

"Since about seventy years ago."

"*What?*"

Mr. Darby laughed, then said, "Tarsiers, mostly. But we use others as well. Our world invades yours once yours falls to darkness."

"Way, way, *way* cool!" said Richie.

Noah steered the topic back. "How many Crossers are people?"

"Not many. Most people are dedicated to the Inside or the Outside. Most don't have the courage to cross."

Richie said, "And what makes you think we do?"

"Seeing is believing."

"Huh?"

"You crossed through Little Dogs of the Prairie, Penguin Palace, and the Chamber of Lights—without even knowing how to! Don't think this happened without the notice of the Secret Council."

"Yeah, but we were—"

"On top of that, we just put you through a test—a test you passed very smoothly, I should add."

"What?" said Noah. "A test?"

"The Secret Metr-APE-olis," said Mr. Darby. "That test was proposed by the Secret Council. I apologize for not announcing it beforehand, but Council insisted that the four of you not know." Mr. Darby glanced at Tank. "How many prospective Crossers would you say fail to cross the Secret Metr-APE-olis?"

Tank smiled, and his perfect teeth gleamed like pearls against his dark skin. "Don't know. But most of them, that's for sure."

Mr. Darby turned back to the scouts. "Not many people have the emotional strength to swing across a forest from the arms of apes, I assure you. Yet, the four of you crossed with ease. Most didn't think you would." Mr. Darby gestured toward Sam and his companions. "Even our young Descenders doubted your ability."

Noah wondered if this was partly why the Descenders didn't like them—because the scouts had proven them wrong.

"Hold on," Ella chimed in. "Your Crossers don't seem to be doing such a great job of things. Nobody stopped *us* from sneaking into the Secret Zoo a few weeks ago."

Mr. Darby laughed and said, "That's because the animals protecting the sector gateways wanted you in—to find Megan and solve the mystery of her disappearance. Think about it. The prairie dogs, Podgy, Blizzard, Little Bighorn—they're all Crossers, and they all wanted you inside."

"That makes sense," said Megan. "But what about me? I was able to sneak in."

"Which made only the second time our borders were breached," said Mr. Darby. "Not so bad, given our history."

"Who breached your borders the first time?" Richie asked.

Mr. Darby frowned at the thought. "We're about to get to that."

Megan shifted the conversation back, saying, "How come I wasn't noticed when I came through the Chamber of Lights? Who was guarding that exhibit?"

"Charlie Red," Mr. Darby said. "And I assure you, his work is normally exceptional. But that day, Charlie had stepped away from his post to investigate a noise outside the exhibit and accidentally locked himself out! It was fifteen minutes before another Crosser could leave her post to unlock the door. By that time it was too late. You were in."

"So that's why he can't stand us," Ella said. "We made him look like a dork."

"Perhaps there's some truth in that," said Mr. Darby. "No one likes to look incapable of doing his job."

A moment passed without question or comment. Then Mr. Darby continued. "Regarding our Crossers, we need more humans. We especially need people to concentrate on the Outside—people who can walk our borders in the Clarksville Zoo without raising eyebrows. People who know the surrounding neighborhood, its residents and properties. People who can cross quickly into the Secret Zoo during an emergency."

Megan chuckled nervously and said, "Mr. Darby . . . we're kids! We have families. And school."

"Yeah," said Ella. "I have to think that life gets pretty tough for someone who quits the books in fifth grade."

Mr. Darby leaned over his knees. "We aren't suggesting that you give up your lives. Only that you help us in your free time—that you train with us and be alert for unusual activity on the Outside, especially in your neighborhood. Our ability to watch activities on your streets is limited, especially during the day."

"Train with you?" said Ella. "Do you have any idea how hard it was for Megan just to get permission to come to the zoo this morning?"

"Training wouldn't take the time you might imagine," said Mr. Darby. "Maybe two hours, twice a week. Much of the training would take place in the Clarksville Zoo, making it that much easier for you."

The scouts glanced at one another and silently considered the proposition. Noah thought about how the Clarksville Zoo was in their neighborhood, right between their houses and their school. After a bit, Noah asked, "How would it work?"

"The Secret Council has proposed that Tank lead your training. He'll be assisted by the Descenders. Sam, Tameron, Hannah, and Solana are four of the strongest, most capable Crossers we have. You would train slowly, on weekends, evenings, or any days that you have available."

"But what would we tell our parents?" Ella asked. "How would we get out of the house?"

Mr. Darby looked at Tank, whose smile was broader than ever. The big man reached into a duffel bag beside his chair and pulled out a wad of shirts in the clutch of his massive hand. One by one, he tossed a shirt to each of the scouts. "You'd say this."

Noah opened his shirt and laid it on the back of Blizzard's head. A button-up with vertical stripes, it had an enormous collar that reached across the shoulders. The left side had two patches; one had the words CLARKSVILLE ZOO in loopy cursive writing, and the other read NOAH. The right side had a breast pocket large enough to fit a *Harry Potter* paperback. It was the ugliest shirt Noah had ever seen.

"Coooool!" Richie gushed as he opened his shirt and buried his entire hand in the pocket. "It has a ton of space for my pens and stuff!"

Ella rolled her eyes. "A nerd and his nerd gear."

"What would we do with these?" Noah asked.

"You'd work for us," said Mr. Darby. "Only a few hours a week, of course."

Richie raised one eyebrow. "You wouldn't . . . like . . . expect us to clean the cages or something, would you? I mean, the elephants! Have you seen the size of their . . . you know . . . poop?"

"You don't get it, Richie," Noah said. "Mr. Darby doesn't want us to work for the zoo. He wants us to make it seem like we're working for the zoo. We'll actually be training."

"Exactly!" Mr. Darby said. "We call it crosstraining. But to your families, we could easily mask it as volunteering. As you probably know, the Clarksville Zoo offers volunteer opportunities to students at the local schools. It's a perfect way to present your training as something acceptable to your parents."

"How long would the training take?" Noah asked.

"Since you'd only be training a few hours a week . . . a number of years."

"Great," said Ella. "There goes my soccer career."

Tameron suddenly stepped forward. "I can't take this anymore!" He faced Mr. Darby, waved an arm toward the scouts, and said, "They're just kids! Kids from the Outside—which is even worse! Yeah, they can cross— I'll give them that—but they don't have what it takes. They haven't seen what we've seen. They're not Insiders,

Mr. Darby. They weren't here the day the shadows were taken!"

Tameron fell silent. As he turned away, the sunlight struck his jacket at an unusual angle. Noah noticed that the pleats had thin cuts in the bottom of the folds. He wondered if there was a reason for the cuts, but before he had time to study them, the Descender moved out of the light, and they were concealed once more.

A prickly silence hung in the air. It was the first awkward moment the scouts had shared with Mr. Darby.

Finally, Noah voiced what all the scouts were thinking. "What did Tameron mean by 'the day the shadows were taken'?"

Tank shifted nervously in his chair. Hannah stopped blowing air into her bubble, and the pink globe seemed to float in front of her face. The prairie dogs stopped racing and stood on their haunches, their attention switching from Noah to Mr. Darby and back again.

Sam took a step toward Mr. Darby and said, "You don't have to answer that. Remember, we're talking to Outsiders here!"

Mr. Darby turned toward Sam and their eyes locked. For a moment, all that seemed to exist was the contemplative aura about the old man. The splashing water in the fountain made the only sounds.

Finally, Mr. Darby turned and faced the scouts. "If

you wish to know the history of the stolen shadows, it will require your full engagement in our plight. We will need you as Crossers, and we will need you not only to be brave, but to be fearless." Mr. Darby paused, giving the scouts time to digest his words. Then he continued. "I want you to think before answering. Can you accept this challenge? The challenge is to become one of us. To join our society as Crossers. Crossers who live on the Outside."

In silence, the scouts traded glances, their eyes communicating more information than words ever could.

At last, Noah said, "If it means helping you—and if it means helping others—then, yes, we accept your invitation to join the Secret Society."

Megan, Ella, and Richie nodded in agreement.

Solana turned to Mr. Darby and said, "You can't be serious! They don't know what they're getting into. They're kids! Think of their parents! What if their parents—"

Mr. Darby raised his palm to silence her. The corners of his mouth curled in a smile, and the old man tipped his head at Noah to show his gratitude. Sitting atop a dreadfully powerful polar bear, Noah nodded back.

"Then, welcome." The usual emotion had drained from Mr. Darby's voice. "Welcome to our Secret Society."

Blizzard rolled back his head and roared so thunderously that the earth shook, the bookcases rumbled, and every creature in the library held on to branches or furniture to keep from falling. Leaves rained down, flashing vibrant color across the magical landscape.

The old man smiled—a smile that was both warm and wicked. He wrestled his aged body into a comfortable position in the chair. Then he set his eyes on the scouts and began to tell a tale.